He touched his lips softly to Rachel's, leaving her breathless

She pulled away from him, trying to regain some ground. Nothing was happening the way she'd planned. Her control had abandoned her. She definitely wasn't acting like the sexy, ice-queen seductress she'd planned to show everybody in town.

His eyes beckoned. She swallowed. Only hours ago she'd have been thrilled to leave this man crumpled on the sidewalk, starved with unrequited love for her. Decked out in a black knit bodysuit, thigh-high leather boots and bloodred lipstick, she would have just stood there, one foot propped on his stomach in victory, while she casually filed her nails.

The best laid plans...

A chill coursed up her spine, and she shivered.

He closed his arms around her. "Tell me, what do you want?"

She swept her tongue over her lips, longing to taste him. There was no question what she wanted—what she needed—right then.

In his eyes, she could see he wanted her, too.

Then it hit her. *She had him right where she'd wanted him!*

Dear Reader,

When Rachel Dean showed up as a secondary character in *Nobody Does It Better*, I knew this was a woman who had to have her own story. But it wasn't easy coming up with a premise as outrageous as Rachel herself. That got me thinking. What if Rachel wasn't always so outrageous, so confident, so...sensual? Now, there was a story....

In *Reckless*, I sent Rachel Dean, former-wallflower-turned-bombshell, back to her small Texas hometown to exorcise some personal demons. Ten years ago three high school seniors had made her prom the worst experience of her life. Now Rachel's come back— smarter and sexier—and she wants revenge. Her plan? To make those three men absolutely crazy with lust for her...and then leave them drooling in their desire.

Only, she ends up seducing the wrong man....

I sure hope you enjoy Rachel and Garrett's story. I'd love to hear from you. You can write to me at P.O. Box 15111417, Austin, TX, 78715-1417, or visit my Web site at www.juliekenner.com.

Happy reading,

Julie Kenner

Books by Julie Kenner

HARLEQUIN TEMPTATION
772—NOBODY DOES IT BETTER

RECKLESS
Julie Kenner

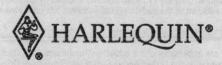

TORONTO • NEW YORK • LONDON
AMSTERDAM • PARIS • SYDNEY • HAMBURG
STOCKHOLM • ATHENS • TOKYO • MILAN • MADRID
PRAGUE • WARSAW • BUDAPEST • AUCKLAND

To Stephen Carver and to Sam Bernstein,
both wonderful friends—then, now and in the future.
Your unwavering support has meant so much to me.
But you already knew that, didn't you? Love you guys!

And, again, to my editor, Brenda Chin,
for making the year 2000 one of my very best!

ISBN 0-373-25901-8

RECKLESS

Copyright © 2000 by Julia Beck Kenner.

1

THREE MEN. Three seductions. One reunion.

Perfect.

For fifteen hundred miles, Rachel had been tweaking the details of her plan.

It would work. *It had to.*

Biting her lip to keep the tears at bay, she tightened her grip on the steering wheel, slowing as she approached the Braemer city limits sign. Her image stared back from the windshield, dark hair and pale skin reflected against a velvet black sky.

Straightening her shoulders, she sat up straight, determined to be the woman she'd become. Attractive. Successful.

Confident.

She'd made something of herself in the past ten years. And over the next few days, she'd prove it.

To them...and to herself.

By the time she headed back to New York, she'd be even with the Three Stooges—Derek Booker, Jason Stilwell and Carl MacLean. The boys who'd made high school a waking nightmare.

She nibbled on her lower lip. Surely no one in town would even recognize her now. Fat, shy Belinda Rachel no longer existed. She was just Rachel now, and this new Rachel looked good. No, not just good. *Hot.*

She had panache, dammit. Sex appeal.

The new Rachel had the right ammunition to tempt, tease and tantalize the Stooges until they were desperate with lust—desperate for *her*. She'd string them along until the reunion dance. Then she'd tell everyone who she was, and let them know the Stooges just weren't good enough for Rachel Dean.

A renegade tear trickled down her nose, and she wiped it away, irritated that her cool Manhattan facade had crumbled from nothing more than a look around the town square. She never cried. *Never*. Apparently the tears hadn't gotten the memo, because they didn't seem to be clued in to the whole no-crying thing.

A bolt of lightning ripped the sky. Almost instantly, raindrops pummeled the car, their *rat-a-tat* on the metal roof almost deafening. The county road intersected Main Street and she turned onto the square, squinting to see through the deluge. *Useless*. With a frown, she pulled into a parking space and killed the engine, then settled in to wait out the storm.

A flash of green and gold caught her eye, and she reached into the passenger seat to finger her invitation to Braemer High School's class reunion. If someone had told her ten years ago that she'd willingly come back, she never would have believed them. Yet here she was, practically drowning in memories of a hell more commonly referred to as high school.

Senior year had been the worst. That year, Carl had started to shield her from the other kids' jokes and catcalls. Then his buddies joined in and she'd let herself believe the Three Stooges were her protectors, maybe even her friends.

When the prom rolled around, she'd learned how foolish she'd been. Carl invited her, and—like an idiot—she'd accepted. For the occasion, she'd scrimped and saved, bought a dress that actually fit and styled her hair. Her mom had even called in sick to her second job and had done Rachel's nails.

She'd waited, stomach in knots, palms sweating, in the dimestore-decorated living room for Carl to pick her up. She hadn't expected romance, but neither had she been prepared for his cold silence as they drove to the dance. Then, once inside the crepe-paper decorated gymnasium, he'd left to find punch. It must have been a scarce commodity, because he'd never come back. And when Rachel told Jason Stilwell and Derek Booker that Carl had invited her, Jason had laughed in her face.

The climax of her humiliation had been when Jason climbed on stage and announced that the class had voted her the Girl Most Likely To Die A Virgin. At the time, she'd desperately wanted to be a character in a Stephen King novel—ideally, Carrie. But Cujo would have been fine, too.

Lightning split the sky, and she cringed.

She'd run away and hadn't looked back. A week later, she'd arrived in New York. By a year later, she'd reinvented herself.

But as much as she'd tried, she hadn't escaped Braemer by running away. No matter how hard she fought, no matter how thin she became, no matter her wit, her charm, her makeup, her money—nothing ever changed. For ten years, Braemer had colored in gray every success, stealing the pleasure from every minor victory.

Well, no more. It was time to confront the ghosts of her past and get on with her life.

"Virgin queen, my tushie." She'd make the Stooges want her more than they'd ever wanted any woman. And in the process, she'd get back the life they'd stolen.

Truth be told, if the invitation had arrived two weeks

ago, she probably would have tossed it. But it had come on the heels of two miserable weeks surpassed only by her years in Braemer.

She'd lost the lease on her Manhattan apartment, learned that a book deal she'd spent a month negotiating had gone sour, lost an appeal in a trademark case that could have put her small law practice on the map, and gained two and a half pounds.

But the big kicker—the *pièce de résistance*—was getting dumped by her current dinner-date-and-dancing boyfriend.

Everything had been going along fine. She'd actually been seeing him for over a month. Then suddenly—*wham!* Somehow he'd seen past the chic veneer and under the designer clothes to the insecure, fat little girl with glasses, braces and frizzy hair. And he hadn't wanted that girl.

Well, who would?

Stop it! She slammed her palm hard against the steering wheel. She'd changed. Exercise, clothes, hair, makeup. Attitude. She'd mixed all of it together and created a whole new image, a whole new persona. She was the one in control. Not the boys. *Her.* If high school had taught her anything, it was to grab the upper hand, and never let go.

And that's exactly what she intended to do.

The hammer of rain had slowed somewhat, so she started the engine and backed the car out. She maneuvered out of the square and onto the county road, hoping the Cotton Gin was still the local hangout.

She frowned, not really in the mood to turn on the charm. After all, without a raincoat or an umbrella, she'd look like a drowned rat. Maybe she should just go back, check into the bed-and-breakfast, and skip the Cotton

Gin altogether. Chances were Carl wouldn't even be there. If she didn't find Carl tonight, was she willing to search out Derek Booker?

Nope. Carl MacLean was Intended Testosterone Overdrive Victim Number One. If Rachel was going to sashay back into town with the aura of a sex kitten and the mentality of a slash-and-burn general, she had to get off on the right foot. That meant going after the Big Dog. This was her mission, after all.

Yes, indeed. She wanted Carl first.

But right now, she wanted to stay dry. Maybe just for tonight she could postpone her mission and curl up in bed with a good book. That is, if she could get to the B-and-B before the steady *thwack, thwack* of the wind-shield wipers drove her insane.

Determined not to be hypnotized by the drone of the engine and the wipers, she leaned forward, her chest pressing against the steering wheel, and tried to see past the rain pounding against the windshield.

Then she saw the dog sitting in the road.

She spun the steering wheel and slammed on the brakes, which probably was a mistake, because the car fishtailed, hitting the lump with a sickening thud. Tears welled in her eyes. Whatever it was, it was alive.

Rachel pumped the brakes. Useless. The damn car was going to take its own sweet time coming to a stop, which it finally did when its front end ran into a ditch.

She was out of the car in seconds, running into the road. A dog. A big, black dog. A Labrador, maybe.

Had she killed it? As if to reassure her, its eyes opened, and it thumped its tail. Just once.

Rachel's chest tightened as she remembered Dexter, the yellow mutt who'd adopted her the summer after sixth grade. He'd been as loyal as he was scrungy-looking.

And this fellow...oh God, he was looking at her with huge, soulful eyes just begging her to help him. She kneeled down next to the poor thing, only then realizing that his hindquarters were, well, bloody. Oh man, oh man, oh man. What had she done?

As she petted its muzzle, the dog licked her hand. Running her fingers through his fur, she checked for a collar, a nametag, something. Nothing. He was her responsibility, and she didn't have a clue what to do. She started to stand up, planning to ransack her suitcase for something to wrap the poor thing in, but the second she pulled her hand away, it whimpered.

Wet and hurt on a dark road. No wonder it was whining. "It's okay, baby. I've just got to get something to put around you."

The dog whimpered again, and Rachel knew she wasn't going anywhere. She couldn't bear to let go of the poor thing. With one hand on its head, she stretched her arm, hoping she could reach the trunk. Not hardly.

"Okay, big guy. Here's the plan." With her left hand, she fumbled at the buttons on her sheer Versace blouse, finally giving up and just pulling until the buttons popped off and the shirt hung loose over her camisole. She shimmied out of it, only realizing how soaked she'd become when the material stuck to her skin. "I'm gonna put this around you and carry you to the car, and then we're going to go scour the town for a vet."

Her size eight blouse wasn't enough to swaddle a full-grown dog. That brilliant realization was soon followed by another—one woman, even a woman who'd kicked off her lucky black pumps—couldn't pick up a wounded dog of this size. So much for that you-could-buy-a-house-with-these-payments gym membership...

"Oh, sweetie, I'm sorry, but I can't lift you." The big guy licked her hand, and Rachel almost cried. She kneeled down and studied his mottled fur. If she pushed him to the car, would she make his back leg worse? Maybe if she could bandage it somehow.

But bandages weren't exactly dropping from the trees. In fact, she didn't have a damn thing. Frustrated, she glanced down, scowling at her now-soggy panty hose.

Not great, but it would have to do.

GARRETT SPRAWLED on the leather couch in his brother's law office and waited impatiently for Carl to get off the phone. The overworked air-conditioning had decided to go on the fritz and the trickle of tepid air did little to combat the Texas heat. It hadn't faded with nightfall, and Garrett had peeled off his button-down shirt, leaving him clad in only a thin white T-shirt, three for five dollars from the drugstore near his house.

He probably should have expected the heat and the uncooperative air-conditioning. From the moment he'd arrived in Texas, Garrett's day had kept getting worse and worse. First his plane hit the edge of the storm front and spent twenty minutes imitating one of those carnival rides he hated. Then, still queasy from the turbulence and carsick from the ride into Braemer, he'd been roped into standing in for his father, the county's answer to James Herriott, and aiding a foaling mare with a breech birth. Even though it had been exhilarating, now his eyes were gritty from lack of sleep, and every muscle in his back and shoulders was screaming at him to get some rest.

Standing, he tapped out an unfiltered cancer stick,

then slid it between his lips, ignoring the plastic No Smoking sign on his brother's desk.

Carl covered the phone's mouthpiece with his hand. "I thought you quit years ago," he said, the comment more an accusation than a question.

"I did quit. But when I'm irritated, I like having one." Garrett eyed his kid brother. Now that Garrett had passed the thirty mark and Carl was approaching it, the family resemblance had increased. Garrett still had a good three inches over Carl, but both had the lanky build and dark coloring typical of MacLean men. Looking at Carl, Garrett saw a reflection of his own finger-combed black hair, along with the unmanageable cowlick that drove every woman he dated nuts when she realized he just couldn't—or wouldn't—look suitably sophisticated in a tux.

Technically, they might only be half brothers, but that kind of bloodline distinction meant nothing to Garrett. Carl was his brother, plain and simple. And when he looked at Carl, he saw himself. He also saw their father.

Nothing Garrett ever did had been good enough for Carl MacLean, Sr. Garrett even became a veterinarian, but the old man had barely even blinked. He sure as hell hadn't invited his oldest son to move back to Braemer and join his practice.

Garrett spread his hand across his forehead and massaged his temples with his thumb and middle finger, trying to shove aside his melancholy mood. Carl hung up the phone, staring at the cigarette. "Don't worry," Garrett said. "I don't light 'em."

"Kinda James Dean like, huh? Just sorta hangs there on your lip and flops around while you talk."

Garrett grinned despite himself. He never could stay mad at Carl. "Fine. You win." With painstaking deliberation, he took the cigarette out of his mouth, slipped it back into the package, and tucked the damn thing into the hip pocket of his jeans.

He managed the entire maneuver without ever taking his eyes off Carl, then waggled his eyebrows for effect. "Let's see how long you can stay in the winner's circle." He dropped into the hard wooden chair across from Carl's desk, leaned back, and thrust his legs out. He kept his focus on Carl, who was fighting a grin of his own, no doubt getting into their old game just like Garrett.

Garrett linked his fingers together and stretched his arms out in front of him, then behind, before letting his head rest against his interlocked hands. Still he didn't say a word. Just stared at Carl the way he'd done when they were kids. The Great American Stare-Off. Garrett had never failed to win.

This time was no exception. Carl squirmed in his chair, then finally broke eye contact. He threw up his hands, the grin spreading to his eyes. "Okay, okay," he said, then chuckled. "You win. Man, some things never change."

Garrett frowned, the comment reviving his earlier mood. "I don't recall you ever lying to me before, baby brother."

Carl pulled a pencil from the chrome cup on his desk and tapped the eraser against the ink blotter. "Look, I can see why you're irr—"

"Did I say I was irritated? That was a mistake, because dammit, Carl, I'm not irritated. I'm not even annoyed. I'm completely, totally, one-hundred percent pissed off."

Carl raised his hands in surrender. "I'm just the messenger."

"The hell you are."

Carl looked away, apparently fascinated with a potted palm in the corner of his office. Garrett watched his brother inhale, saw the familiar tic in his cheek as Carl worked out in his head how to get what he wanted from his adoring older brother. And why not? For the kid's whole life, Garrett had willingly coddled his every whim. Big brother and best friend rolled into one.

When Carl was five, he'd wanted Garrett's collection of *Star Wars* action figures. When he was ten, he'd wanted Garrett's old helmet and a real football. At thirteen, he'd wanted Garrett to stay and not go away to college.

That was the only time Garrett had turned his brother down. With everything else, he'd been putty in the kid's hands from the day baby Carl had come home from the hospital. Yes, indeed. Garrett would do just about anything for Carl. But he had a sneaking suspicion he'd been lured back to Texas under false pretenses. "Look, you want to tell me why I was shanghaied into running interference for Dad's practice only a millisecond after I pulled into town?"

After a pause long enough to swallow a hippo, Carl turned back to face him. "The old man needs you. He wants your help."

Garrett knew better. His dad had never wanted him, much less his help. Too bad for Garrett, he'd been born to the first wife. The one his dad *had* to marry. The one who'd skipped town right after he'd been born.

He reached for the cigarette pack, realized what he was doing, and grabbed hold of the armrest. "You're not telling me something. What?"

"Why would I lie?"

Well, that was the question of the hour. And Garrett didn't have a clue. He pushed himself out of the chair and started pacing Carl's neat-as-a-pin office. He stopped in front of the University of Texas Law School diploma, remembering how proud he'd been watching Carl get that sheepskin. With a sigh, he gave in to the urge to rummage for his cigarettes. "Why now?"

"Garrett, I—"

"I'm supposed to just forget everything? All because he snapped his fingers? And you? You just jump when he says 'boo'? Did it ever occur to you that maybe I have a life now in California?"

"You've told me a thousand times you miss Texas."

Garrett frowned, not in the mood to give in to logic. "So? Maybe I don't want to come running back here just to help the old man keep his podunk vet practice running." Disgusted with the situation and himself, he balled the cigarette pack and heaved it at Carl's trash can. He missed. "And you up and lied to get me here."

"Garrett, calm down."

"I am calm. This is me being very, very calm."

Carl took off his glasses and put them on his desk. "You're right. I lied. Sue me. But he can't handle the calls with a thrown back, and I knew you wouldn't come for him. I took a chance you'd come for me."

Garrett let out a long breath. "You know I'd never turn my back on you." That's why Carl's lie had rankled so much. Without a second's hesitation, he'd dropped everything to give his brother a hand. Would he have come so quickly if he'd known his dad needed help? Maybe. Maybe not.

Would he have come if his dad had been the one doing the asking?

Definitely. The truth of the answer gnawed at him. He'd spent the past thirty-some years praying his dad would do something, *anything*, that showed he cared about Garrett, even a little. Now here he was, laid up with a bad back, and he hadn't even asked his son—a trained veterinarian—for help.

"It's not just about Dad," Carl said. "There're the animals, too."

"That's hitting below the belt."

"Nah, just taking advantage of your soft heart."

Images of the animals drifted through Garrett's mind. No way his dad could've foaled a mare in his condition. Hell, laid up in bed and zonked out on painkillers, the old man couldn't even tend a kitten. And unlike Garrett, who had a thriving specialty practice in the Malibu Canyon, Dr. Carl MacLean, Sr. didn't have a staff of eight.

Damn. Well, maybe he would stay and help, at least until he could line up a replacement. But he didn't have to like it.

The phone rang, and Carl picked it up. "Carl MacLean... Hey, Liz... A committee? I don't think so.... It's just that I'm not even sure I'm going to the reunion.... No, just...uh, work stuff... Yeah, I'll call if I change my mind. Bye."

"You're not going to your reunion?" Garrett asked the second Carl hung up the phone. "Why wouldn't you go? You won all those awards, got all those scholarships. You should go."

"Who are you, my other father?" Carl avoided Garrett's eyes, his fingers tapping time on his desk blotter. "I've got stuff to do."

There it was. Lie number two. The first lie, that Papa MacLean wanted his help, Garrett could live with. Without Garrett, the practice really would go under. And Carl was right, Garrett wanted to help, if for no other reason than the animals.

But this new lie...

The Carl he knew had loved school. He'd been popular, a jock, and welcomed by the cool kids. So why would a kid who'd practically walked on water during school, and who was now a successful lawyer, not want to go to his ten-year high-school reunion?

Not for the first time, Garrett regretted leaving Texas after graduation. Keeping up with his brother from California had been difficult, and he'd missed a chunk of Carl's growing up. "You want to tell me why you're really not going?"

Carl exhaled loudly, then rubbed his face with the palms of his hands. "Maybe later, okay? For now let's just say I did a really dumb thing, and she left town before I could apologize, and I've regretted it for the past ten years."

"Who?"

Carl gave him a look.

"Who?" Garrett repeated.

Carl sighed. "Belinda Dean."

The name didn't ring a bell. "Do I know her?"

"She was my year. Not a real attractive kid, you know? We razzed her pretty good." He looked up. "You met her at least once, though. Dad fixed up her dog right before you left town."

Garrett nodded, pretty sure he remembered. "Shy girl, never looked you in the eye?"

"That's her."

"I got her to laugh."

"Well, you were the first in the entire town, then. She was practically in a cocoon through all twelve grades. Only person she ever hung with was Paris Sommers, and Paris and her dad moved away after junior high."

"So what did you do to her?"

"I wanted to make friends with her, actually. I thought she could use one. But Jason and Derek had other ideas and I got swept along in it." He shrugged, managing to look both pitiful and resigned. "I don't want to talk about it. Okay?"

Garrett nodded, clenching his fists at his sides and biting back the urge to lay into his baby brother. If he'd needed any more proof that he should have hung around Braemer, the fact that Carl had gotten himself mixed up with bozos like Jason and Derek did the trick.

"You want to stay at my place?" Carl asked.

"No, I've got a room. Thanks, though." He walked to Carl's office door, then turned back and aimed a warning finger. "But we're not through, little brother. You got me here under false pretenses. And now whatever you're not telling me about this Jason and Derek thing... Plan on downing a six-pack tomorrow and spilling your soul to your older and wiser brother. Deal?"

Carl half grinned. "Sure thing, O Wise One."

Garrett crossed the darkened reception area, flipped the lock, and pulled open the front door to Carl's office. A rush of night air accosted him as he stepped onto the porch of the remodeled Victorian-style house.

Gravel crunched under his boots as he hurried to his father's four-by-four that Carl had borrowed for him, softly cursing the rain that seemed to have settled permanently over Braemer. The dankness matched his foul mood, recently made worse by Carl's newest lie, and the hidden truth. Tomorrow he'd get the full story. Most likely it was just kid pranks. Stupid stuff only Carl remembered.

In the truck, he dialed his dad's number on the speaker phone, hung up before it could ring, then dialed again. His stepmother answered.

"I'm coming by to see Dad," Garrett announced before he could talk himself out of it.

"Carl said you were back in town."

"Hi Jenn," he said, backtracking into normal conversation. "I hear Dad's laid up. I'm coming by," he repeated.

"I'd love to see you, of course, but there's no sense driving out here tonight in this rain. Your dad's not home."

Garrett gaped at the speaker. "I thought his back was out."

"He's in Temple. Tests. I took him there this morning."

So much for acting on impulse. They said goodbye, and he clicked the phone off, part of him relieved he'd have a day or two to prepare for the inevitable moment when his father would just look at him and wish him a nice trip back to California. A *go away kid, you bother me* kind of moment.

With a groan, he slammed his palm against the steering wheel and pushed his father out of his thoughts, concentrating instead on driving through the rain. Damn, it was coming down hard. He hoped Mrs. Kelley's B-and-B had plenty of hot water. The last thing in the world he wanted tonight was an ice-cold shower.

He was still contemplating the plumbing when he saw the woman in the road.

Now *there* was a reason to take a cold shower.

Shirtless, her lacy camisole was drenched and stuck to the curves of her breasts. That alone would have been enough to convince Garrett to pull over. The fact that she was standing in the middle of the road waving at him was more or less secondary.

He rolled down the truck's window and slid to a stop

beside her, grateful the rain was starting to let up. "Need a hand?"

"Not at all," she said, shooting him a you're-an-idiot look. "I always hang out in the rain in my underwear. It's invigorating."

Garrett had to grin. He'd deserved that zinger. For that matter, he welcomed it. Lately he'd been bored out of his mind dating agreeable, wanna-be actresses who never argued or even voiced an opinion for fear they might offend him and his wallet. So running across a spunky woman, even in a decidedly non-date situation, actually put some of the silver lining back in his otherwise dreary day.

"Are you going to sit there staring at me and my wet clothes, or are you going to get moving on that help you so chivalrously offered?" The woman glanced pointedly behind her and Garrett noticed the Lab, who joined in the conversation with a thump of his tail.

"Right," he said, killing the engine and hopping out of the truck. With her second sarcastic remark, his bad mood had fizzled away, and now he hummed as he knelt down next to the dog and probed the injured area. "Hey, big fella." He pushed away the makeshift bandage and studied the dog. He'd need some X-rays, but from what he could tell, other than a sprain in his front leg and several nasty-looking abrasions, the big guy was in pretty good shape.

He sat on the pavement, one hand rubbing the dog's ears, and looked up at his smart-mouthed beauty. She wiped the drizzle off her face and looked back at him, her brow furrowed, as if she'd just met him at a party and couldn't remember his name.

"So, what happened?" he asked.

She blinked, and her face cleared. "Does it matter? The point is, I need to get him to a vet. Soon."

"At your service. We can take him to my clinic," he said, trying to gather the dog in a way that wouldn't hurt his back or the dog's anything. Then he realized what he'd said. *His* clinic? Thank God, Carl wasn't around to hear that one.

"You're a vet?"

He grunted, struggling to stand with a load of wet, injured dog. "No, but it seemed like the perfect pickup line under the circumstances."

"Sorry. Stupid question."

Well, well. Score one for Garrett's team. If he weren't lugging the dog, he would've pitched at an imaginary hoop and racked up two points. But he was carrying a dog. A heavy, wet dog that was getting heavier by the second. He cleared his throat and nodded at the tailgate of the truck.

"Oh." She rushed to open it. "You're sure he'll be okay?"

He slid the dog in, then pulled a tarp out of the toolbox and draped it over him. "He's going to be fine. Not too much blood lost, doesn't seem to be in shock. I'll check out that leg, clean him up, give him a couple of stitches and he'll be back chasing cats in no time."

"I want to stay with him."

"Fine." He nodded toward the sedan sitting at the side of the road with its headlights on. Presumably it belonged to her. "Just follow me into town."

"It's stuck."

"Then you can ride with me. I'll call for a tow truck," he said, adding a silent thank-you to the rain gods. He noticed the ruts in the muddy shoulder. "You lost control and hit the dog?"

She nodded and looked down at the pavement.

"Are you okay? Did you hit your head?" Without thinking if she'd mind, he hooked a finger under her chin and lifted her face. A quick look at the pupils of her dark brown eyes satisfied him that she wasn't in shock. But the tears welling up showed him only too well how much the accident had rattled her.

"I wasn't going that fast. But I didn't see him," she said, sniffing. "And I didn't know what to do with him." A tear streamed down her already wet face, but she made no move to wipe it away. "I never cry."

"So I see." He brushed the tear away, surprised at the warmth of her skin. "You did fine. And he's not hurt that bad." He looked at her bare legs. "I don't think I'd have thought of using panty hose to wrap a leg."

She let out a soft little laugh, and he reveled in the sweet sound before silently cursing himself. The last thing in the world he needed was to get the hots for some woman while he was half a continent away from Los Angeles.

"I was a Boy Scout in another life," she said. "Be prepared and all." She lifted a shoulder, and the camisole moved over her breasts. Garrett held back a groan, but wasn't stupid enough to look away from her taut nipples grazing the silky white material. She'd blow away the competition in a wet T-shirt contest.

"Here," he said, shrugging out of his slicker and handing it to her.

"I'm fine."

Maybe she was, but he was decidedly un-fine. "This isn't a point for debate, sweetheart. Put the jacket on."

Her mouth twitched. She was either fighting back a smile or an argument. But neither came, and she slipped it on. She was a tall woman, almost as tall as him and he just passed the six-foot mark. Even so, it swallowed her. She looked like a kid playing grown-up, her bare legs and feet the only part of her not covered by his rain gear. Vulnerable. Innocent. He wanted to help her.

Hell, he just plain wanted her. The realization unnerved him, and he chalked it up to the endless stream of deathly dull dates he'd had in the past few months.

She walked to the ditch and pulled a purse from her car, shutting the headlights off before slamming the door. Then she followed as he circled the truck and opened the passenger door. "Nice truck," she said, peering in over his shoulder at the mess. The tears were gone, replaced by the light sarcasm he already considered her trademark. Garrett smiled, knowing he must have soothed her fears about the dog.

He swept his arm along the passenger side of the bench seat, carving a place for her to sit from among his dad's veterinarian journals, old coffee cups, fast food containers, shotgun shells, and God knows what else. *Thanks, Dad. Always count on you to help me make a kick-ass first impression.*

Of course, his dad didn't use the truck to pick up women, so in fairness Garrett had to cut him some slack. The old man practically lived in the pickup, spending his afternoons driving between ranches spread out over the Texas Hill Country, checking in on the horses, pigs, cattle, cats and dogs he treated. Hell of a lot more satisfying than the administrative garbage Garrett put up with day in and day out.

The mess didn't faze his passenger. She climbed right in, not even needing his gentle push against her back to boost her into the cab. Inside, she grabbed a towel hanging from the gun rack and spread it out as a makeshift seat cover.

He circled the truck and joined her. "Sorry about the clutter."

"Considering the day I've had, it's only appropriate."

He cranked the engine, then glanced at her, but she didn't explain, just tilted her head and smiled. What a smile. The kind that could get under his skin if he wasn't careful.

He cleared his throat. "Rough day?"

She twisted in her seat and looked out the back window. "I thought so until I hit him." The corner of her mouth lifted in a half smile. "That sort of shifted my perspective around, if you know what I mean."

With one hand, she pushed her hair away from her face and leaned her forehead against the glass. "You're not just being kind? He'll really be okay?"

She looked so vulnerable, so scared, that he wanted to pull the truck over, take her in his arms and rock away her troubles. Since that was about as likely to happen as a flock of monkeys flying by on their way to Oz, he opted for flat-out honesty. She seemed to need it, and he never cut corners with the truth. At least not where his animals were concerned.

"Look," he said, "I'm not a miracle worker, but I don't think he needs a miracle. I could be wrong, though. I won't know for sure until I get some X-rays and can see him in better light, but from what I saw and felt on the road, I really think he's going to be just fine."

He could almost see the tension melt out of her shoulders. "Thanks for being up-front with me." Whiskey smooth, her voice filled the cab of his truck, surrounding and caressing him. There was something comforting about the lilt of her voice, the cadence of her speech. Something welcome.

"I'm glad you stopped to help me." She flashed a

sweet smile, but looked down before he could return it. Was his passenger the shy type? She picked up one of his dad's vet journals and toyed with it in her lap. "Anyway. Thanks."

"You're welcome," he said.

The corner of her mouth twitched, and she settled back into her seat, crossing her legs. The slicker fell open, revealing one of the legs he'd noticed earlier. He stifled a groan as he remembered the pantyhose she'd used on the dog and wondered if she was wearing anything under that short, tight skirt.

His throat parched and he swallowed. *Cool it, Mac-Lean.*

She was counting on him to be her chivalrous knight. So now was not the time to be thinking about her voice, her legs, her smell, *her anything.*

Now was the time to drive.

2

A WARM DRAFT from the truck's not-quite-closed window grazed her bare skin, and Rachel realized the slicker had fallen open. She uncrossed her legs and yanked the coat closed, not ready to face the fact that fate had jump-started her plan by sending Victim Number One to her rescue. But there was the proof, right in her lap. She tried to keep her hands from shaking as she studied the mailing label on the veterinary journal.

Carl MacLean, D.V.M.

Trying to be unobtrusive, she turned slightly, studying his profile out of the corner of her eye. Before leaving Manhattan, she'd pulled out her senior yearbook. She'd always assumed Carl's image had been permanently burned into her mind, but his class picture brought back little details she'd forgotten. Like that wayward lock of hair that still hung over his right eyebrow.

No question about it, she and the dog had been rescued by none other than Intended Testosterone Overdrive Victim Number One. She nibbled on her lower lip, remembering the press of his hand on her back as he helped her into the truck, her skin still tingling with the memory of his innocent touch. Considering that she shivered from nothing more than a casual touch, how would her body react if he touched her with purpose, if her testosterone overdrive plan actually worked?

The thought unnerved her. Something told her that

she could lose herself in his touches, and the last thing she wanted was to crave Carl MacLean. For her plan to work, she needed to be the one in control. The whole point of her trip was to make him lust after her. To make him want her so badly it hurt. And then to just walk away.

"Nervous?"

"Nervous? About what?" she managed, her voice sounding like she'd been snacking on coarse sandpaper.

He cocked his head toward the truck bed, indicating the dog. "We're almost there."

She stifled a sigh of relief. "The dog. Yes, I'm nervous about the dog." That, at least, was an honest answer. She turned in her seat and looked out the window at the lump under the black tarp.

"I wouldn't recommend it, but if it'll make you feel better, you can watch when I fix him up."

Watch? She wasn't sure she could do that. Rachel leaned closer to the glass, her hands pressed against the side of her face to block out the reflection of the truck's interior. She thought she saw the dog stir under the tarp, but decided it was only the wind.

"Thanks, but I'll just wait." Not only could she not bear the thought of seeing the poor dog's untreated wounds, but the idea of Carl as a competent and caring vet disturbed her, threatening to overtake the image she'd already fixed in her mind. An image she needed to hold onto if she intended to go through with her plan.

Already he'd erased part of the mental picture she'd drawn of him. Not once had she anticipated that Carl MacLean might have developed a chivalrous side. But as she stared into the truck bed, searching for any hint that the dog was okay, something tugged at her memory, urging her to realize she'd known all along that Carl could be kind when he wanted.

She remembered the day so many years ago when her dog had been injured. Dexter had decided to take on a momma raccoon, and the raccoon had won. Whimpering, Dex had belly-crawled up to where Rachel sat reading in the vegetable garden, his yellow fur bloodied, deep gashes slashed across his nose and hindquarters. She'd been twelve and alone, her mama in town working at the café and trying to make ends meet. She'd tried to pull him to town in the wagon she'd had since kindergarten, when Carl and his older brother—Gary or Cary or something—had taken pity on her and given her a lift to their dad's vet hospital.

Blinking back tears, she turned around and concentrated on the magazine in her lap, needing to steel herself against the memories, unwilling to let in anything that might redeem Carl. Whether he could be chivalrous simply wasn't the issue.

For that matter, *Carl* wasn't the issue. And neither was Derek Booker or Jason Stilwell. She wasn't coming back to see if they could be redeemed. She was coming back to prove something—to them and to herself. She needed to keep her purpose firmly in mind and not be swayed by a kind word or gentle gesture.

When he reached over and put his hand on her shoulder, she almost yelped.

"Hanging in there?"

She turned, noting the obvious concern reflected in his clear blue eyes. "I'm fine. Really." Even through the thick vinyl slicker, she could feel the warmth of his hand. Knowing she'd regret the broken contact, but needing the distance to clear her head, she scooted away from him and pressed herself against the passenger door. He got the hint, dropping his hand from her shoulder to the gearshift. Immediately, she wished she hadn't pulled away. The whole reason she'd come back to Braemer was to flirt, to tease and taunt Carl and the others. Not to cower in the corner like some wallflower. Like Belinda Rachel.

Either Carl or Braemer was messing with her head, and that was a sensation she didn't like at all. She'd washed off the dust of Braemer when she'd walked away ten years ago. The fact that Carl might be mildly appealing—or even wildly sexy—didn't change anything. She'd come back with a plan, and she had the tools to see that plan through.

She sat up straighter and scooted back toward him, inching even closer than she'd been before. She was Rachel Dean, after all. She could make men drool with a well-placed look. She knew every chic bar, restaurant and dance club in Manhattan. And she never, ever lacked for a date.

Once again, this time with purpose, Rachel crossed her legs. She intentionally coaxed the slicker open, revealing her leg from toe to midthigh. Tilting her head to look at him, she licked her lips, then smiled. "So...where's your clinic?"

As she'd hoped, his gaze followed the curve of her leg. He swallowed, slowing without stopping at Braemer's only traffic light. "Just about five miles this side of town."

She nodded, remembering the MacLean property. The family house sat back, almost a mile from the main road, while the stone clinic faced the major roadway. She turned back and looked at the dog hidden in the bed of the truck. Surely he'd be okay for a few more minutes.

Carl caught her eye and flashed a reassuring smile.

Automatically, she smiled back, a genuine smile without any hint of Manhattan Rachel behind it. She sighed. With the dog weighing on her mind, she was having a hard time focusing.

Just past the far edge of town, Carl pulled into a service station and parked the truck under the overhang.

"Gas?"

He opened his door. "Let's check on your friend."

When he stepped out of the truck, she followed suit, moving around to meet him at the tailgate.

"MacLean? That you?"

Carl waved at a grizzled old man standing just out of the rain in the station's doorway. Rachel almost gasped. She knew that man. Elwood, Elmo, something like that.

"Hey, Elmer. Just stopped to check something in the truck."

Elmer. Of course. The crusty mechanic who'd taught her how to air up her bicycle tires. She turned away, facing toward the truck. Chances were Elmer wouldn't recognize her, but why press her luck?

"Need a hand?"

"Thanks, but I've got all the help I need," he said, waving in Rachel's direction as he hopped up into the bed.

The old man grunted, stepping back into the building as Carl reached for her wrist to hoist her up.

She let him pull her into the truck bed, then found herself pressed against the hard breadth of his chest, his free arm wrapped around her waist. Concentrating on keeping her breathing normal, she tried to ignore the delicious pressure of his body against hers. *Impossible.* Gently but firmly, she pushed away, silently urging him to release her. "I…I'm going to check on the dog."

Kneeling down, she peeled a bit of the tarp back. The

Lab opened its eyes and yawned, licking her hand when she reached down to stroke its muzzle. Carl bent down beside her, pulling the tarp further back to reveal the dog's injured hindquarter. The Lab whined a little while Carl probed the area, but otherwise behaved, finally thumping his tail when Carl pulled the tarp back up to its neck.

Scratching the dog's ears, he grinned at Rachel. "Patient's hanging in there."

"You still think he'll be fine?"

"Yup." Carl tucked the tarp around the Lab and stood up, reaching down to help her to her feet. "I think he'll do just great."

Rachel relaxed and let him help her down. Twice now he'd reassured her that the dog would be fine, and she'd seen the Lab just now with her own two eyes.

In the truck, she leaned her head against the back of the seat, taking deep breaths and exhaling slowly. The inevitable pressed against her. The dog would be fine. She'd made it to Braemer. Neither Carl nor Elmer had recognized her.

And Carl, her very own Victim Number One, was about to open the driver-side door and slide into the truck cab.

She'd come back to Braemer with a purpose, and all her excuses had evaporated.

It was time to turn on the charm.

One by one, she undid the snaps on the slicker. As his door opened, she slid toward the middle of the bench seat, letting the coat fall open, again revealing quite a bit of leg and now adding a subtle hint of camisole. She smiled as he started the car. "If I haven't already said it, Dr. MacLean, thanks for helping us out."

DR. MACLEAN? Even as she said his name, Garrett tried to remember if he'd introduced himself. He looked at her out of the corner of his eye, caught a glimpse of leg and lace, and swallowed. "Did I introduce myself?"

She licked her lips. "No, you didn't."

He frowned. "Okay. So...have we met?"

"Are you suggesting you might have forgotten me?"

"Sweetheart, I'm sure I'd remember you." That was the understatement of the year. Something told him that in only a few short moments this woman had already burned herself into his memory. If he was the romantic type, he'd say she'd etched her image onto his soul.

"Thanks. I'll remember you said so." She turned in the seat to face him better, revealing more of those long, silky legs in the process. He wondered if they were as smooth as they looked. "Actually, we knew each other in high school. At first, I wasn't sure it was really you." She flashed that smile again. "I was hoping I'd see you on this trip."

High school? He glanced at her again, but found no spark of familiarity. Of course, he was lousy with faces and high school had been a million years ago. "So how'd you finally recognize me?"

"Does it matter?" she asked in what he assumed was her bedroom voice, low and velvety. Designed to entice. She was playing some sort of game with him, but damned if he knew the rules. Didn't matter. He could play his own games. Keeping light pressure on the accelerator and his eyes on her, he waited.

"It helps if you stay between the little lines in the road." Garrett kept watching her. And kept right on driving through the drizzle. A mental game of chicken.

She held his gaze, then looked at the road and back to him, a small smile playing at her mouth. "You win," she said, patting one of his dad's journals on the seat between them. "Subscription. Mailing label. Funny, but I would have sworn you'd ended up in law school."

Law school? Why on earth would he have gone to law school? Then realization hit, slapping him across the face with more force than a jilted lover.

She thought he was Carl.

He eased off the gas and turned in his seat, planning to explain away her misunderstanding. Then he caught her expression, along with all the carnal implications hiding in her liquid eyes.

"I didn't go to law school," he said. It wasn't a lie. But it wasn't exactly the truth, either.

"No? Well, guess that means I'm not psychic. Just nosy." Her pink tongue slid over her lips as she slid closer, moving her leg to straddle the gearshift.

Her hip pressed against him and Garrett's stomach dropped, the last remnants of his good intentions running for the hills. He wanted her. This woman who thought he was Carl. Whose beauty intrigued him and whose spunk aroused him. A woman totally unlike the women he'd left behind in California.

He focused on driving, trying not to let her warmth distract him. Clearly he'd been thrown for a loop. He needed to keep his head and not tumble into something he—or she—would regret.

She held up one of his dad's magazines and rifled the pages. Leaning over, she whispered. "Now are you satisfied?"

Garrett concentrated on keeping both hands on the steering wheel. "Not entirely."

"No?" She grabbed the rearview mirror and twisted it toward her, then pulled a tube of lipstick from her purse. "Well, be sure and let me know what I can do to help...satisfy you." She pursed her mouth and smoothed the soft color over her full lips, then turned the mirror back toward Garrett, capping the motion with a wink. He didn't bother to adjust it. He was still imagining everything she could do with those lips.

Damned if she wasn't coming on to him. No, not him. *Carl.*

He really should clear up her mistake. Tell her he wasn't Carl. Let her run this little seduction number for his brother. Yup, that's what he should do. And that was a damn shame.

Especially after the day he'd had, the thought of throwing this prize Carl's way really got under his skin. It wasn't as if he'd be stepping in on Carl's action. Hell, the woman didn't even really know Carl. She could even be a gold digger. He'd be doing his brotherly duty by keeping her away.

Give it up, Garrett. At least call a spade a spade. You're interested. Very, very interested.

When he shifted gears, he used the motion as an excuse to take another look at his unexpected passenger. She'd turned her head slightly to look out the back window. Now her forehead was creased with concern and perfect white teeth worried at her full lower lip. Even like that, the woman was sexy. No, this way she was even more alluring than when she was intentionally flirting. For reasons he didn't understand, this vulnerable woman was hiding behind a sex kitten routine.

For the second time that night, he itched to take her in his arms and kiss away her troubles.

Wasn't that exactly what she was offering him?

No.

Whatever she had in mind, Garrett didn't think it involved getting close—truly close—to him or to his brother. The smart-mouthed, innocent, sexy woman he'd stopped to help wasn't running the show. For some reason, she'd turned on a Mata Hari routine. Sultry. Hot. Alluring. And distant as hell.

She caught him watching and the coy smile reappeared.

He turned away, not quite able to meet her eyes. *Damn.*

He thought about the hell he'd been through getting back to Texas. About spending hours mired in mud. About Carl tricking him and then not giving him the full story. About busting his back over the upcoming weeks to keep his father's practice afloat, even though he knew the old man wouldn't thank him.

He thought about the rain and his exhaustion and the generally crappy mood this woman was managing to lift. Just for one night he wanted to lose himself with her, to lock his reality out until morning.

So go for it. She's flirting with the man driving the truck— you. She's just got the name wrong.

He grinned. *That which we call a rose...*

"What's so funny?"

He looked up. "What?"

"You're smiling."

"I was just thinking about what a hypocrite I am."

"Oh?"

"I've been trying to think of a justification for flirting back. Something more noble than that I just plain want to."

He tapped the brakes, slowing as he approached the turnoff for the clinic.

"Flirting back?"

"You've been flirting with me."

"Have I?" She looked away, but Garrett could see her smile in the reflection on the glass. "I suppose I have."

She ran the tip of her finger along his thigh, the contact almost burning a hole in his jeans. He downshifted, the side of his hand brushing her smooth skin. "Is that okay, Dr. MacLean?"

Garrett had to bite back an ironic laugh. A soaked-to-the-skin, sexy-as-hell woman had practically dropped from the sky into his arms. And she wonders if it's okay to flirt? He pulled in front of his father's office and killed the engine. "I think I can handle it, Miss..."

"We should get the dog into your clinic."

So she didn't want him to know her name. Odd. But considering she didn't know his name either, that made the whole deal a little bit better from his point of view.

A lump of guilt melted as he opened the door and stepped out into the damp night air. A whirlwind fling wasn't his usual thing, but his life wasn't particularly usual right now. Neither was this woman. She excited him. Made him think the kind of thoughts he'd avoided for a long, long time.

He had no idea what her agenda might be. But if he had to get close to the little temptress to find the woman underneath, well, he'd just have to suffer through.

And he did want to see where this would lead.

After hours of pure hell, and despite the never-ending drizzle, his evening was starting to look up.

RACHEL GULPED as he peeled off the plain, white T-shirt that didn't seem plain at all on this man. Try as she might, she couldn't draw another breath until he pulled the scrub top down and covered his washboard stomach. She'd read that term in books. Now she knew what it meant.

Without a doubt, her efforts to get him all hot and bothered in the truck had hit the mark. Too bad for her, she hadn't anticipated her skills boomeranging back on her. But that's exactly what had happened.

And now here she was, standing in the cheery reception area amid posters of cats and dogs, clutching the scrub shirt and pants he'd given her, her blood burning hotter than sin.

His smile when his head appeared through the V-neck suggested he knew exactly what direction her thoughts were heading. She frowned and tried to look aloof. *She* was supposed to be the one seducing *him*, after all. Not the other way around.

He cocked his head toward the open door behind him where the dog lay. "Want to whisper sweet nothings before I get this show on the road?"

The man was devious. Did he know how his double entendres affected her? Mentally, she shrugged. Of course he did. That was the point. But she intended to beat him at his own game.

And have a hell of a good time doing it.

She raised an eyebrow, a trick she'd mastered after spending too many enraptured hours watching Mr. Spock. "Sweet nothings?" She stepped closer and trailed her finger down his arm, enjoying the way his jaw tightened as if he were fighting for control. "Is that what you'd like me to do? Whisper?"

"To the—to the dog," he said, coughing slightly. "I thought you might want to say something to the dog."

She looked over his shoulder at the Lab, sprawled like a soldier on the cold table, waiting for Carl to make it better.

"Hey baby," she called, and the dog thumped his tail once in response. He was a trooper, that dog. His stamina coupled with Carl's skill, and he was sure to be fine. She frowned, wondering why she knew that Carl was an excellent vet. But it didn't matter. She was sure. And right then she was grateful.

Glancing back up at Carl, she smiled. "Just a quick word, and then you'd better get started."

With a wave, he ushered her into the operating area. Scratching the dog's ears, she bent close. "I don't really know this guy, but I've got a good feeling. You'll do fine." She rubbed her nose on his scruffy muzzle, and he licked her chin.

"Okay," she said, standing back up. "Guess it's time for you to work your magic." She pressed her lips together, trying to bring the right words to mind. "You'll make him better, right?"

He smiled, blue eyes crinkling, as he reached out and tucked a strand of hair behind her ear. "Don't worry."

As he leaned closer, her pulse pounded and she struggled to take what should have been an easy breath. His lips brushed her cheek, leaving fire in their wake. Realization smacked her in the head, and she knew she'd gotten in way too deep.

When he eased away, she almost whimpered. When he pulled a syringe from a drawer underneath the steel table, she stiffened. "I think that's my cue to get out of here."

"I'll be as fast as I can."

She smirked. "Don't rush on my account."

Grinning, he looked fondly at the dog. "Don't worry."

Waving her hand in the direction of the door, she started backing out of the room. "So. I guess I'll just wait. Out there." She eyed the syringe. "Where it's safe."

"Take a nap if you want. There's a lounge in the back.

Through the first examining room. The couch is older than I am, but it's comfortable in an uncomfortable sort of way."

She shook her head. "I don't think I can sleep. But at the same time, I'm not sure I can stay awake. It's been a long day."

"Coffee. My fa—my assistant has a coffeepot, I think. Just scrounge around and see what you can dig up." He started to close the door, blocking her out. "A cup of coffee when I finish this doesn't sound half bad, actually."

"No?"

He chuckled. "Maybe I'll get lucky and some passing female will take pity on me."

"If your passing female's of the stranded variety, it's the least she can do."

She'd meant it as an innocent comment, but from the gleam in his eyes, he'd twisted her meaning around. In one step he was at her side, his finger hooked under her chin. She tilted her head back and saw determination and a hint of passion in his eyes.

"If that's the least," he whispered, "I'm very interested in discovering the most." Then he brushed his lips over her cheek, stepped into the operating room, and shut the door.

Rachel just stood there, her hand pressed to her cheek, trying to pinpoint the exact moment when she'd lost control of the situation.

Not that it made any difference right now. He was behind that door, and she was the last thing on his mind. By the time he finished with the dog it would be well past midnight, and he'd certainly need some caffeine. So she'd be June Cleaver and go start a pot of coffee.

As she filled the carafe with water, she couldn't help but grin. *Domestic* would have been the last adjective she'd pick to describe how she intended to behave once she got back to Braemer. But here she was, making coffee and wondering if he had any cookies stashed away, because surely he'd be hungry, too. And the truth was, this brush with domesticity felt kind of nice.

But as she poured the water into the coffeemaker, she had to wonder if she'd still be able to pull off her plan.

3

RACHEL PACED in front of Carl's operating room. She took a swig of coffee and wondered what was going on behind the door.

He'd sworn the dog would be fine, and she actually trusted him. A week ago she wouldn't have believed it. But now...

The suspense was killing her. She moved closer and spoke through the door. "Is he okay?"

"As okay as he was when you asked me two minutes ago."

"Right. Sorry." At least he sounded amused and not annoyed with her incessant questions. She ran her hands through her hair and continued pacing. If someone had told her that Carl had grown up and joined a motorcycle gang, the news wouldn't have rocked her world. But to discover that the boy who'd destroyed her self-esteem had grown up into a spokesman for Be Kind to Animals Week...well, that was a little much to take in.

What had she been thinking in his truck? Coming on to him then had been silly. She'd been frazzled, off her game. Not that he'd noticed. On the contrary, if it hadn't been for the dog, she probably could have jumped him in the truck. It lacked an element of class, and it certainly wasn't her style, but the thought of this new Carl and her on the bench seat, fogging up the windows and putting the shock absorbers to the test...

She shivered, the thought making her insides go watery.

Get a grip, girl. The plan was not—repeat, not—to fall for Carl. This was a one-way seduction. True, his unexpected appearance had saved her butt, not to mention the dog. But he'd put a huge kink in her plans. Trying to make him all hot and bothered while she was frazzled about the dog and looked like one of Dickens' orphans had been a major setback. Her plan needed the right clothes, the right hair, and tons of attitude.

She'd have been better off waiting until she was wearing makeup that wasn't smeared and clothes that weren't crumpled and damp. Until she wasn't reduced to shaking fits every time she remembered hitting that dog.

She pictured the poor dog looking at her and thumping his tail. *Thumper.* That's what she'd call him.

She rubbed her hands vigorously over her face, trying to stay awake, then plopped down hard on the bench and stared at the closed door. What was going on in there? Antsy, she got back up and moved closer, about to shout through the door yet again. She caught herself. *That* would be a smooth move.

Instead, she pressed her ear against the door. Not that it made a difference. She couldn't hear a thing.

When the door flew open a second later, Rachel jumped back.

"For crying out loud, you scared me to death." She stood there like an idiot taking deep breaths to calm down while Carl leaned against the door frame watching her, amusement apparent on his face.

She patted her chest. "Okay. Okay, I'm calm now. How is he? How's Thumper?"

"Thumper?"

She looked over his shoulder into the room.

"Oh, right. Thumper'll be just fine."

"Really?" She pulled herself up so she could see straight into his eyes. Pale blue like Paul Newman, and he didn't blink once. Okay, good sign. He wasn't jerking her chain.

"Really." He put his hand on her arm. A friendly, supportive gesture that had a much-more-than-friendly effect on her insides. "How are you? Still shook up?"

Shook up? That was putting it lightly. She was operating on almost no sleep, had practically drowned in the middle of the road, had barely missed killing a dog, and had ended up splattered with mud and street grime. Then, to top it off, her knight in shining armor turned out to be none other than the man she'd come all this way to seduce and reduce to a crumpled pile of male ego.

The same man who was standing before her looking, well, yummy. And she looked like she'd failed Intro to Hygiene.

"Miss?"

She stepped back, silently urging him to let go of her arm. "I'm fine. Fine. Really."

His gaze raked over her. "Well, you do look mighty fine."

A wry smile tugged at her mouth as she glanced down at the shapeless, puke-green scrubs he'd given her to change into. "Just keeping up with the Paris fashions. I'd hate to be caught in the wrong outfit."

"I'm betting the wrong outfit would look just right on you. For that matter, it would probably look even better off you."

Oh, Lord, she could actually feel herself blushing. Where had that come from?

The whole night was not going as she'd expected. Somehow Carl had managed to grab the upper hand in their little game. Unacceptable. Rachel Dean did not lose sex games. Certainly not to a man who wasn't even in her league.

Straightening her shoulders, she flashed her sophisticated city-girl smile, the one that never failed to catch the men.

"Are you flirting, Doctor? Or offering?"

"Well, now, I guess that depends."

"On what?"

His smile just about stopped her heart. "On which answer will keep you around longer."

Oh, my. She took a shaky breath. With what seemed like very little effort, he'd turned her insides to mush. And mush was not the proper frame of mind for her plan of attack. She needed to get her head back on straight. To be the one in control. The script in her mind cast her as the Seductress and him as the Lowly Luster. But Carl was on a completely different page. In his performance, he was the Handsome Stranger, and she was the Cowering Maiden whose heart was thumping wildly.

That wouldn't do, and she scrambled for safe territory. "Can I see Thumper now?"

Her ploy worked, and in an instant, he transformed from available hunk to concerned vet. "Follow me."

The operating room opened up to a kennel, and there was Thumper, zonked out in a cage that seemed plenty big, but broke her heart anyway. Something brushed her leg and Rachel looked down into the single eye of an otherwise beautiful calico cat.

"Blinky, meet my mystery guest. Blinky's been here

forever. She keeps the place running. Does night patrol. Greets visitors. That sort of thing."

Rachel leaned down to give Blinky a head-scratch, which, if the way the ancient cat purred was any indication, meant they were now friends for life. "Hey, kitty."

"She keeps everyone in line."

"Tough job, I imagine."

"Not me. I'm pretty much housebroken." He flashed a lopsided grin. "You can take me anywhere."

Take him? Oh, yeah, she could take him.

"Is that an invitation?"

"Would you like one?" He'd pitched his voice low, and her knees went weak.

Say yes. Say yes and go see what kind of mileage you can get out of that couch in the back.

She looked at the floor. "Why don't you let me pet Thumper," she mumbled.

Inside her head, New York Rachel was screaming a blue streak. In Carl's kennel, the ghost of Belinda Rachel had possessed her body and tied her tongue.

Carl opened the cage and she rubbed Thumper's head. The weary dog opened his eyes and blinked, then nuzzled her hand before drifting back off to sleep.

Those damn tears threatened again, but this time they were tears of relief. Rachel opened her eyes extra wide, fighting them back. "Thank you so much. I don't...he couldn't...."

"It's okay," he said, reaching for her.

She struggled to keep from jumping at the surge of feral awareness that shot through her when he casually stroked her cheek. When she realized he'd brushed away a tear, the floodgates opened and she sobbed, letting him pull her into his arms and hold her tight. With her face buried in his shirt, she sniffed and blustered like an idiot, realizing only after the fact that she'd practically adopted his shirt as a handkerchief.

So much for her attempt to be the world's greatest seductress. Another sniffle and she willed the faucet to stop. Carl pushed her gently away and looked down at her. She met his eyes and quirked a smile, hoping he didn't think she was a basket case, and absolutely certain he wasn't going to fall prone at her feet, knocked over by the strength of her sex appeal.

"Are you all right?"

"Stressed, tired, relieved. Everything. But I'm fine."

His lips brushed her eyebrow. Just a quick touch, nothing really. Yet still enough to leave her breathless.

Nothing was happening as she'd planned. Control had abandoned her. If there was a sexy, tempting, tantalizing ice-queen seductress anywhere nearby, it sure wasn't Rachel.

His eyes beckoned, warm and friendly, but with longing as well. She swallowed. Only hours ago she'd have been thrilled to leave him an empty shell crumpled on the pavement, starved with unrequited love for her. Decked out in a black knit bodysuit, thigh-high leather boots, and blood-red lipstick, she would have just stood there, one foot propped on his stomach in victory, while she casually filed her nails.

The best laid plans...

Now she wanted his comfort, his touch, and she cursed herself for falling so easily to his charms. She never fell this fast. Never.

Hell, she never fell at all. She was always too busy making sure she had the upper hand, making sure the men saw only the Rachel she wanted them to see. In all of ten years, she'd only let one man get even remotely close, and he'd dumped her. So much for opening her heart to the world.

A chill coursed up her spine, and she shivered.

Carl closed his arms around her. "Are you cold?"

She shook her head. Burning up was more like it.

His lips danced over the top of her ear, the stubble of his beard grazing her temple. Her pulse quickened, and she reminded herself to breathe.

"Is someone expecting you?" His voice was hesitant, a whisper. "Do you want me to take you somewhere?"

"No," she said, her voice imploring, begging him not to take her anywhere. To just *take her*.

"Good," he murmured. "What *do* you want?"

She swept her tongue over her lips, longing to taste him there. There was no question what she wanted— what she needed—right then. Right there.

From his eyes, she could tell he wanted her too.

Then it hit her. *She'd won.* Mission accomplished and they hadn't even achieved liftoff.

Somehow, despite the soggy clothes and the smeared makeup, she'd maneuvered him exactly where she'd wanted him. Breathless and hard and wanting her so bad it hurt.

This was her cue. She should just walk out the door and move on to victims two and three. Then, at the reunion—in front of everyone who'd witnessed her own humiliation—she'd reveal her true identity. Simple.

She took a breath, reminding herself of why she'd come all the way back to Texas. Her mission, remember? The plan was to leave Carl MacLean so desperate he hurt. And to make sure he knew that Belinda Rachel Dean was the one who'd got him that way. Trouble was, right now walking away would punish her as much as him. Every atom in her body glowed like an ember, ready to ignite. And, Lord have mercy, she needed him to stoke that fire.

If she walked away in the morning, she'd still prove her point. Maybe even better, right? Then he'd really know what he was missing. And she'd get to have her proverbial cake and eat it, too. Sure. Not a problem.

A little voice disagreed, telling her that sleeping with Carl MacLean would be a mistake. A huge, mind-numbing, screw-all-her-plans kind of mistake. Maybe the voice was right.

But what the hell.

"I want you."

GARRETT EXHALED, realizing he'd been holding his breath. He couldn't remember when so much had hinged on the answer to one simple question. She wanted him. It was a damn good thing, too, because he was pretty sure he'd keel over and die if he couldn't have her. Soon.

He traced the V-neck of the extra-large scrub shirt he'd given her to wear, urging it lower until it revealed the swell of her breast. Then he let his lips take over, kissing her smooth skin, thrilled by the whisper of her breath in his hair.

There was no tan line to follow, and he wondered if she sunbathed topless. Visions of her laid out on a sandy beach haunted him. The sun washing over her bare breasts. Beads of sweat trickling down her cleavage, to her belly button, and even further where his mind had no business going. Not yet. Not if he wanted to last more than five seconds.

Garrett pulled back, and she whimpered. The noise satisfied him enormously. At least he wasn't the only one who'd been broadsided by lust.

He traced his finger over her lower lip, and she opened her mouth for him, her tongue twirling over his skin while he tried to keep a grip on sanity. She kept her eyes closed, and for some reason that made it all the more arousing. She was just standing there, as casual as you please, her shirt pulled down almost far enough to expose her nipple, dark brown hair falling over her eye, suckling his finger.

The sensation fired his arousal. He hadn't been this turned on by a woman in a long time. A very long time, and the heady power of his own lust was a little overwhelming. But not at all unwelcome.

Now she was watching him, her dark eyes dreamy and inviting. "My knees aren't working real well."

"Mine either."

He eased her backwards until she was leaning against the wall, his arms splayed out around her. She was just a few inches shorter than him, which gave him perfect access to her full mouth when she tilted her face up.

Accepting the invitation, he leaned forward, and she moved to meet him, taking his mouth in hers with a hunger equal to his own. If ever a woman could drive him crazy from kisses, this was the one. A virtuoso kisser.

Her mouth played him like a fine instrument. Gently at first, but firm enough that he could tell she knew what she was doing, then building and building to a crescendo that threatened what little self-restraint he had left.

Her hands stroked his back, tentative at first, and then with increasing intensity. He kept his hands on the wall, afraid that if he touched her now, on top of everything else, he'd lose control and take her right there. That wasn't what he wanted. Not tonight. Not with her.

He'd never met such an enticing woman. Her boldness surprised and aroused him. Her teases intrigued him.

He'd make tonight last until tomorrow if possible. And the next day. And the next.

He shook his head. What was he thinking? This was a fling, remember? Her fling. Anonymous, decadent, and oh-so satisfying. But even as he thought it, some part of his mind rebelled. She might have an agenda, but he didn't have to follow it.

She tugged at his shirt, pulling it free from his jeans. "You're too dressed," she whispered. "I'm practically naked here thanks to your oversize scrubs."

"Practically and naked aren't quite the same things."

"Keep on like this and we'll get to actually pretty soon."

He kissed her. Deep. "Promise me."

A smile tugged at her mouth, and she slid her hand around his thigh to his crotch, cupping the erection that strained behind his jeans. Garrett gasped, calling on every ounce of willpower not to lose control right then.

"I promise," she whispered, stroking him—and kindling ideas of things to do to her once she kept that promise.

The wall was doing a nice job of keeping them both from spinning out of orbit, but Garrett had to let go anyway, at least long enough to hit the switch and kill the overhead lights, leaving only the yellow glow of a nightlight plugged in behind the workstation. Never before had he thought a dollar-fifty plug-in light to be anything more than functional, but tonight he would have sworn it was more romantic than candlelight.

"You're beautiful."

He couldn't be sure, but he thought she blushed, and

the idea made him smile. Considering what they were about to do—hell, what they were *doing*—he hadn't expected her to blush like a virgin. He wanted to let her know how special this night was to him. How special she was. "I don't usually do this."

"Pay a woman a compliment?"

"Actually, that either. But what I meant was this," he said, running his finger from her lip, down her chin and between her breasts. He slid his hands under the material and cupped one breast, then teased her nipple with his thumb. "I'm not in the habit of making love with stranded women I pick up in the middle of the night."

"No? Well, I'm not in the habit of getting stranded. But I have to say it hasn't been too bad so far."

He rewarded her sass with one light kiss, then bent down to kiss her breast, his tongue playing at where his thumb had been.

"You're making it difficult to breathe," she said, but her hands intertwined in his hair and pushed him even closer.

"That's the idea," he said as he switched to give her other breast equal attention. She waylaid his plans, pulling him up to her mouth and planting another mind-numbing kiss on him.

"I like your kisses," she said when they came up for air.

"I've never had a nicer compliment."

Thumper whimpered from behind them, and she peered over his shoulder.

"I think we've got an audience."

Garrett grinned. "You have a problem with exhibitionism?"

"I want to adopt that dog. You're about to contribute to the delinquency of a pet."

"Can't have that." He stepped backwards and held out his hand. "Shall I escort the lady to the lounge?"

"How about escorting her to a bed?"

"I'm afraid a lumpy, uncomfortable couch is the best I can do."

Her sultry grin just about stopped his heart. "Right now, that sounds even better than a five-star hotel."

THE WARMTH OF HIS SKIN flowed through her, wreaking havoc with her insides. Even operating on next to no sleep, she couldn't remember the last time she'd felt so awake. The heftiest caffeine buzz in the world couldn't compare to the way her body sizzled just from being close to him. She'd become wanton, wild.

Reckless.

She followed him into the darkened lounge area, eyeing the ugly maroon couch. Carl sat down and held out his hand, and she moved onto his lap with such ease it seemed as if they'd sat that way a thousand times before.

She twisted at the waist and faced him, so close their breath mingled, and their combined body heat threatened to set the couch on fire. His hands roamed her back, their light pressure both steadying and arousing. Even through his jeans and the thin material of her scrubs, she could feel his hardness, knew he wanted her as much as she wanted him. She stifled her smile, reveling in the knowledge that all she had to do was squirm if she wanted to drive him over the edge. Herself, too, for that matter.

She planted a light kiss on his nose. "Not exactly the Ritz, is it?"

"It can be. Just shut your eyes and be anywhere you want to be."

Or anyone?

Who exactly was she tonight? Seductress Rachel intent on making him desperate with lust? Frumpy Belinda Rachel who'd never done anything even remotely like this? Or just Rachel Dean, a woman she wasn't sure she'd recognize anymore if she bumped into her in the mall.

She didn't know. All she knew was that she was moving farther, faster with Carl than she had with any of her endless parade of Manhattan theater-dinner-dancing dates. They'd warranted little more than a good-night kiss even though she'd known they were lusting for a roll in the sack.

With them, she'd wanted just to be wanted.

With Carl, *man-oh-man*, she wanted him.

Wanted him to kiss her, to touch her. Wanted him to quench the frantic passion spreading like wildfire through her body. Lord, she needed him inside her.

The depth of her desire scared her. For years she'd fantasized about payback, and now the reunion presented the perfect opportunity. After all, he and his buddies had set her up, only to send her crashing to the ground.

But tonight...

Tonight he was just a man. A man who needed her as much as she wanted him. A man who craved her in a way he never would have wanted Belinda Rachel.

Finally, turnabout.

He caressed her hair. "Second thoughts?"

Rachel shook her head, clearing her thoughts. "No, none at all," she said, then kissed him, hard, to prove the point.

Tomorrow she could walk away. Tomorrow she'd think about payback. Tonight she just wanted to be the sexy, confident woman she'd tried so hard to project for the past ten years. A woman capable of driving someone like Carl MacLean wild.

Another kiss, this one deeper, designed to leave no question about what she needed. He must have got the message, because he grabbed her hips and urged her to twist around until she was straddling him, her knees pushing into the couch on either side of him. The evidence of his arousal pressed intimately against her and she quivered, moving with a subconscious, erotic rhythm, her feverish longing building with every tiny movement.

Craving the feel of him against her skin, she arched her back, and fumbled at the hem of her shirt, trying to pull it up and keep from falling backwards at the same time. He came to her rescue, his fingers grazing her sides as he pulled the top over her head. The touch was slight, casual and erotic, but still it threatened to undo her.

The rush of air on her naked skin was exquisite. Her already hard nipples tightened almost painfully, begging for his caress. His hands splayed across her shoulder blades, the roughness of his skin delicious against her own. His mouth lowered toward her breast, and she strained forward, needing to shorten the distance between them, desperate for his mouth against her skin.

Heat consumed her, melting her control and firing her passion. His tongue urged her on, whittling away what little composure she had left. Reason abandoned her, replaced by a simple, primitive craving. She writhed shamelessly against him, wanting to press his pelvis closer, harder, deeper against her own. Half of her wanted him to take her over the edge right that very second, and the other half hoped to hang onto the explosion building inside her for as long as possible.

When he pulled away, she whimpered, desperate for

the warmth of his mouth on her other breast. It didn't come, and she opened her eyes, afraid he wanted to stop. One look at his face calmed her fear. Passion clouded his ocean-blue eyes, and his breathing was ragged as her own.

He buried his hands in her hair and looked into her eyes. "Are you staying in Braemer, or just driving through?"

"Right now, I'm happy to just stay here forever. Just give me one of those cages to sleep in during the day and bring me out here at night with you." That didn't exactly answer his question, but it was true. Right then, that second, there was no place else she wanted to be.

He pressed close to her ear. "Consider yourself warned," he whispered. "I'm making it my job tonight to see to it you don't leave any time soon."

She squirmed, biting her lip to hold back a groan when she felt his hardness at the apex of her thighs. "An interesting occupation. Does it come with benefits?"

With casual aplomb, his hand grazed down her back and slid under the waistband of the scrub pants. "One of the best packages I've ever run across," he said, tracing his finger lower and lower until she couldn't stand it and leaned forward, longing to kiss him.

Her body shuddered at the sensation of his mouth against hers. Then he pulled her closer even as his hand slid lower over her backside. When he slipped his finger inside her she gasped, relishing the intimacy even as she craved a bolder touch.

"Do you like that?"

Oh, yes. But she couldn't answer aloud, could only move against him, letting the storm build inside her. She wrapped her arms around his neck and kissed him, her tongue seeking his, drinking in the taste of him.

Some coherent part of her mind reminded her that she never lost control like this, never abandoned herself to a man the way she was with this man. *With Carl.*

Scary and exciting—she couldn't stop to analyze. Not now, not with her wanting more of him, all of him.

She broke their kiss, pulling away slowly. "We still haven't remedied that clothes problem."

He moved his hands to her sides, then slid up to cup her breasts. "No problem here."

She put her hand between them and rubbed his erection that strained against the thick denim. "I'm thinking these jeans and the shirt need to go."

"Funny, I was thinking pretty much the same thing about those scrubs."

Biting her lip to keep her body under control as she disentangled herself from him, she stood up, loosened the drawstring, and let the scrubs fall to the floor. Naked, she settled herself on the couch, her back against the armrest, her legs curled up next to her. Alluring, but modest.

"You're beautiful," he said, moving to lean over her. She closed her eyes, burning from the heat of his exploring hands on her waist, her hips, her breasts. "I can't believe you dropped from the sky just for me."

"Are you sure? Maybe *you* dropped from the sky for *me.*"

He flicked his tongue over her nipple, and she quivered, fighting to keep from begging him to take her right then.

"Either way, I'm a happy camper," he said.

"I'll be happier if you get out of those," she said, trailing her finger down the denim.

"At your service," he said, standing up.

Earlier, she'd seen his naked chest. But that hadn't

prepared her for the perfection of the rest of his body. Tight, muscled thighs and a matching butt that looked damn good in either jeans or scrubs, and even better out of them.

He joined her back on the couch, still wearing briefs and a scrub top.

"This is your idea of naked?"

"I thought you might want to help."

Not a bad idea. Rachel kneeled on the sofa, facing him, and scooted as close as she could, then slid her hands under his shirt, letting her fingers dance on his warm skin as she lifted the material up. When his face was covered by the shirt and his arms were trapped above him, she stopped.

His torso was darker than his legs, and she imagined that he spent a lot of time outside without a shirt, a fine layer of sweat glistening on his bronzed skin. Country life wouldn't be so bad if that was the view out her window every day. A smattering of hair decorated his chest, and she ran her fingers over it, teasing his nipples with the palms of her hands. He squirmed, moving to pull his shirt off.

"Ah-ah. Not yet." Her tongue took over from her hands, and she tasted the salt and inhaled the musk of his skin. With deliberate intent, she littered his chest with slow kisses, working her way down to the waistband of his briefs. His muscles tightened under her touch, and the knowledge that he was fighting for control excited her all the more.

When she slipped her finger under the band of his briefs to stroke him, he groaned and freed himself from his shirt. Burying his hands in her hair, he coaxed her back up to face him.

"A rather awkward thought just occurred to me," he said, then brushed her lips with a kiss.

She had a feeling she knew what he was thinking. "Protection."

"I really doubt there are any condoms here at the office." He tucked a strand of hair behind her ear. "I don't suppose...?"

"Not in my purse." She closed her eyes and dropped her head against his shoulder, silently cursing her forgetfulness.

Well, you didn't plan on getting this far, remember? Just get 'em all hot and bothered and leave 'em lusting.

Unfortunately, she was the one all hot and bothered. For a brief moment she considered walking away right then. Before she went too far and couldn't get back on track.

But her heart wasn't in it. With Carl, she was experiencing something she'd never known as Belinda Rachel. For that matter, she'd never really known passion as Rachel either.

Tomorrow, she'd regroup. But tonight, she needed him.

With one arm hooked around his neck, she pulled him closer. "Don't worry. We'll think of something."

"Yes," he murmured, his breath hot against her ear, "I'm sure we will."

4

GARRETT LOOKED at the woman in his arms and tried to figure out when his common sense had packed up and left for vacation. Probably about the same time he'd seen her standing in the road, her drenched camisole plastered to the curves of her breasts.

Even in his wilder days, he'd never moved this far, this fast. But with her...well, she'd bewitched him, and he'd willingly succumbed to her magic. He wanted to keep her around, see what developed. What better way to do that than to take her over the top, and still keep her wanting more?

"I've got an idea," he said.

"A twenty-four hour pharmacy that delivers?"

He laughed. Man, she was priceless. This was no simpering woman along for the ride. She was just as aggressive about her passion as he was. She wanted him, and made no bones about letting him know. Her obvious desire and distress flattered him. And made him harder than he could ever remember.

"Not in Braemer. Lie down."

She cocked her head, and he could tell she was tempted to argue with him, to play with him. In the end, her curiosity won and she stretched out on the couch, defying him only in the way she propped herself up on her elbows.

"All the way," he insisted, as he moved to kneel over her.

He started with her mouth, touching her only with his lips, then trailed feather kisses down her neck. Except for the slight contact, their bodies didn't touch. Not yet.

When her hands moved to stroke his back, his body warmed and tightened, seeking a release that only she could bring. But that wasn't what he wanted. Right now the moment was for her alone, and he gently moved her hands back to her sides.

"No touching," he said, responding to her silent protest. "Only I get to touch."

She raised her eyebrows but didn't argue, and he reveled in the look of expectation in her eyes.

Her mouth called to him and he turned his attention back to her sweet lips, sucking and teasing until they were swollen and full. *A well-kissed woman.* He moved lower, his tongue tracing a path down her neck, over her shoulder, down the swell of her breast.

When his mouth closed over her nipple, he shifted his weight and moved his free hand to the inside of her thigh. She sighed, her breath grazing his hair. Her skin, smooth and silky under his fingertips, tightened as he stroked the sensitive area.

He heard her suck in air as he moved the ministrations of his hand higher, seeking her heat. His fingers danced along her skin, almost, but not quite, touching her where he knew she longed to feel him. Almost imperceptibly she rocked her hips, and he understood her silent plea for him to end the sweet torment.

"Not just yet," he whispered, releasing her breast and leaning up to see her face flushed with passion.

She moaned, and he lowered himself, pressing her deeper into the cushions of the couch, his thigh over hers, his erection throbbing against her hip. His mouth moved to her ear, his tongue darting and teasing, loving the taste of her, while his hand explored the softness of her leg. He needed her. Right then. Needed to make her writhe beneath him. When she shifted her hips and spread her legs wider to give him better access, he groaned and willed his body to behave.

He trailed his fingers higher, wanting to taste and touch all of her secrets, somehow sure that by claiming the heat she offered, the secret of who she was would be revealed to him.

He cupped her sex, and she quaked when his thumb stroked her nub. His desire to be inside her over-whelmed him, and when he slid his finger into her, she thrust against him, letting him know her need was just as powerful.

She was wet and silky and hot. *For him.*

"Tell me you want me," he said, his voice ragged.

"Yes," she moaned. "Since the second I saw you."

Garrett didn't know if it was true, and he didn't care. Right then, she was ready for him, and he intended to satisfy her as best he could under the circumstances. He wanted this to be a night she'd remember forever.

A night she'd want to repeat, to take further—soon.

She squirmed, sighing and moaning, as he let his fingers concentrate on taking her to the brink. "Yes...don't stop."

He had to smile. He had no intentions of stopping. He'd stay like this as long as she wanted, watching the way her skin flushed under his touch, the way she licked and bit her lip, the way her back arched with each small spasm.

She surprised him by crying out and clamping her

legs together, trapping his hand. She squirmed, her breathing ragged, and pressed harder against him.

He hadn't planned on his own release, but her quick response, so powerful and intense and uninhibited, had brought him to the edge. And over.

When they started to breathe normally again, she spooned against him, and he traced his fingers up and down her side.

"Who knew a vet would have such an amazing bedside manner?" she said, her voice laced with sleep.

He chuckled. Once again, she'd surprised him.

She was a keeper. Not only was his body already addicted to her, but he genuinely liked her—including her smart mouth and quirky sense of humor. He had a feeling life wouldn't be dull with this woman nearby.

The ceiling loomed over him, and he remembered his deception. How on earth was he going to tell her that he wasn't Carl? He exhaled noisily, waiting for a brilliant epiphany.

Nothing. Well, damn.

He glanced over at her profile, relaxed and beautiful now in sleep, a slight smile gracing her lips. He kissed her cheek, surprised by the fierce wave of possessiveness that washed over him. Somehow, he'd figure out a way to break the news. Somehow, he'd make it right.

Of course, he wasn't the only one playing at deception.

On top of confessing his true identity, he still needed to find out her name.

CARL'S ARM DRAPED over her chest, and Rachel snuggled against him, their bodies fitting together, the rise and fall of his chest making her feel safe. Secure.

In the magic circle of his arms, the world made sense.

She was just Rachel. He was just Carl. Two strangers who'd met and sparked a fire between them the likes of which she'd never experienced before.

A fire she had no business letting burn free.

She closed her eyes and sighed. Once she left his arms, the circle would be broken. He'd no longer be just Carl. He'd be the man who'd hurt her. The man she'd come back to humiliate at the reunion dance.

And who would she be? The new Rachel she'd worked so hard to become? Or Belinda Rachel, a girl she'd tried to leave behind, but who she'd been bumping into ever since she rolled into town?

She pressed closer to Carl, seeking comfort in his warmth. Then she realized what she was doing and stiffened.

Oh, Lord, what had she done?

She needed to get away, needed to get her head on straight. She couldn't think in his arms. And if he woke up, if he kissed her, she'd melt under his caress.

Taking care not to wake him, she slid out of his embrace and half rolled, half dropped from the couch to the floor. He moved behind her, and she held her breath. Then she glanced over her shoulder and saw that he'd pulled the blanket up and clutched it to his chest. She smiled, her mind drifting back to the way his arms had held her tight, his touch both erotic and protective.

Trying to be as quiet as possible, she gathered the scrubs off the floor and, naked, crept out of the lounge area, shutting the door behind her. Good manners told her to change back into her own clothes. But when she grabbed her stuff from behind Carl's bathroom door, all her Emily Post good intentions dissolved. She couldn't bear to part with the scrubs. Silly, but she wanted a souvenir of their night.

Back in the reception area, she glanced at the door to the operating room. *Thumper.* He was hers now, her responsibility. If she left without him, she'd have to come back. And that meant facing Carl again. Not something she was sure she could handle.

And Carl did say that everything had gone fine. In fact, just hours after he'd been stitched up, Thumper had already looked one hundred percent better. She'd awakened once during the night, her heart pounding when she realized Carl wasn't beside her. She found him in the kennel checking on the dog. Thumper had been wide awake, eyes bright, even managing to hobble around with one leg bandaged. They'd let him out, and he'd immediately gone to Rachel, covering her face with doggy slurps.

No, she couldn't leave without Thumper.

She tiptoed to the front door and peered through the blinds. Her car was there, right in front. Just like Carl had promised. Good.

She glanced at the clock. Not quite eight. With any luck, Carl wasn't an early riser.

Inside the kennel area, she knelt in front of Thumper's cage, holding a finger over her lips when he whimpered. She lifted the latch and pulled open the door, cringing when it creaked. After waiting long enough to be sure Carl wasn't about to burst through the door, she coaxed Thumper out.

"Now, be very, very quiet," she whispered. "Otherwise, Carl might wake up, and then I'll really be in a fix."

The dog cocked his head, as if he, too, was listening. Then he licked his chops with a pink, wet tongue and made his way toward the door, maneuvering pretty well despite his bound hind leg. He stopped at the threshold and looked back at her.

"I'm coming. Just give me a second." She rummaged in her purse until she found her wallet. For all she knew, emergency dog surgery cost over a thousand dollars. Unfortunately, she didn't have that much cash, and she couldn't leave her credit card, since that would tell him her name. So she left three hundred in cash and hoped Braemer had been dragged into the new millennium, at least enough to have installed an ATM.

As she urged Thumper through the reception area, she noticed the pet supplies lining the shelves. She glanced at the dog, then back to the shelves, then back to Thumper again. She'd just have to mail him some more cash.

"Stay," she whispered, then raided the shelves for a bag of kibble, a collar, and a leash. "Okay," she said, returning to the dog, "let's get this on you." She fastened the collar around his neck, then leaned in to rub his ears and nuzzle his fur. "You're gonna stick with me, right, old boy?" she said, breathing in the comforting smell of dog.

He snuffled, and she took that as a yes. With the leash wrapped around her forearm, she bent over and hooked her fingers under his collar. With her other hand, she flipped open the dead bolt and opened the door. Again she waited, her senses on overdrive, hoping Carl wouldn't hear and come running after her. Silence. She stepped into the morning air, urging Thumper along with her, then pulled the door shut. She couldn't lock it, but the odds of some murderous weirdo stopping into the local vet and finding Carl were pretty slim.

Thumper needed some help getting into the backseat, but after a few hefty shoves, she got him settled. Sliding behind the steering wheel, she tried to get her bearings and remember which direction she needed to go to get to the B-and-B.

According to the Bluebonnet B-and-B's website, Lenora Kelley had bought the historic home five years ago when she'd moved from Austin to semiretire. Rachel had picked it over one of the local motels specifically because Mrs. Kelley was an outsider and couldn't blow Rachel's cover.

She found the place sitting back from the road on about two acres of well-shaded property. Painted blue with white trim, the place seemed both lazy and inviting. It reminded her of the old abandoned farmhouse where she and Dexter had played. She smiled, remembering how she'd pretended the place was hers, even going so far as to pick out paint colors and wallpapers.

Now she peered at the B-and-B. Only two cars were parked in front, and Rachel hoped that meant the place wasn't full. Of course, in a few days, as the reunion dance drew closer, the house would likely be overflowing with her former classmates. Well, she could worry about that later. Right now she needed to worry about her dog.

She got out of the car and opened the back door, then helped him down to the ground. "Now you wait here," she said as she looped his leash though the door handle. "I need to make sure I'm allowed to bring you in."

The inside of the B-and-B was just as quaint as the outside. Rachel found Mrs. Kelley setting up a breakfast buffet in the dining room. White lace tablecloths adorned every table, each topped with a plate and an upside-down coffee cup that reminded Rachel of just how long she'd gone without caffeine.

Rachel cleared her throat, and the older woman turned.

"May I help you?"

"I'm Rachel Dean. I have a reservation."

Mrs. Kelley's face brightened. "Oh, good. I'd expected you yesterday. I was a mite worried when you didn't show up, what with the storm and all. But you're here now."

Rachel bit her lip, not sure she believed that anyone in this town—new resident or not—would spend even two seconds worrying about her. Still, it was rude not to have called, and she managed a small smile and a mumbled apology as she followed Mrs. Kelley back to the entry hall. A massive antique desk served as a reception counter, and the older woman slipped behind it and started tapping away at a computer keyboard.

"It was the rain," Rachel said, feeling like she had to explain. "I, uh, decided to stay in Austin rather than drive through the storm."

"Good thinking. With all the creeks, these roads often flood." She reached to pull something off the printer. "Now, just fill this out, and I'll give you your key. I'm putting you in the Wildflower Room. It's in the back of the house, and it has its own door out to the garden." She began rummaging through a box of keys.

"Perfect," said Rachel. "Do you take pets?"

"No, dear, it's just not worth the extra cost to replace the carpets and clean the upholstery." She looked up, peering at Rachel over the top of her glasses. "Oh, my. Did I forget to tell you that in my e-mail? Do you have a pet with you?"

Rachel started to say yes, figuring Mrs. Kelley would make an exception if she thought the mistake was hers, but the woman continued on.

"I've made arrangements to board pets free of charge at Dr. MacLean's kennel. Do you need me to give him a call?"

"No," Rachel blurted. She wasn't giving Thumper up for anyone. And she certainly wasn't giving him up to Carl. The thought alone unnerved her. "I don't have a dog. I was just curious." She smiled, sure Mrs. Kelley thought she was a loon. "Allergies. That's it. I'm allergic."

Not even twenty-four hours after she'd rolled into town, and already she was acting like a babbling little schoolgirl. She'd definitely lost it.

Mrs. Kelley patted her hand. "Here's your key, honey. Why don't you get settled, relax a bit, then come have some breakfast?"

Relax? Rachel wasn't sure she'd ever relax again. She was wound up tighter than a spring. Not only had she completely sabotaged her own revenge plan last night, but now she had to figure out what to do next. Let Carl know who she was? Or blow him off altogether and move on to Jason and Derek?

And on top of all her other problems, she was about to smuggle a wounded dog into a house where he wasn't welcome. Then she had to convince him to stay quiet and not tear up the upholstery or shed on the linens.

No, if she wanted to relax, she should head back to New York and take a midnight stroll through Central Park. Because in Braemer—with Carl on the brain—she had a sneaking suspicion she wouldn't be doing any relaxing for a very long time.

EVEN FROM WITHIN the grip of sleep, Garrett knew she had gone. He willed himself awake, already saddened by the loss of his mysterious temptress. With a groan, he rolled onto his back and linked his fingers behind his head, staring at the ceiling and wondering what the hell he was going to do now.

Options bounced around in his mind. He ruled out the Texas Rangers right away. For one thing, he wasn't positive Texas still had Rangers. Even if it did, he doubted that tracking down seductive women was within their jurisdiction. No, best to blow off the Rangers and move on to option number two—combing every restaurant, motel and guesthouse in Braemer. And if that failed, then maybe he could trace the license plate of her car. Surely Ernie must have written it down on some form or other when he towed it in last night.

He propped himself up and swung his feet to the floor, trying to ignore the one final option that moseyed through his head—*forget about the girl.*

No. The response screamed through his brain. Maybe foolish, definitely selfish, but until he knew for certain she was gone, he intended to hang onto the hope that he'd find her.

And maybe in the meantime, he'd figure out what he was going to say to her.

He grabbed his clothes off the floor and pulled them on. Exhaustion spidered through his body, his arms and legs tingling from jet lag and lack of sleep. He rolled his head in slow circles, trying to work out the kinks. According to his watch, it was nine-thirty, three hours later than he usually woke up.

Not surprising, though, considering how little sleep he'd gotten the night before. He smiled, remembering the curvaceous, sexy, adorable reason he'd been awake for so much of the night. Then he frowned, remembering the other reason—the furry, slobbering one. Her Thumper.

It had taken a massive effort to leave the cocoon of warmth they'd created, but he'd crept into the kennel last night and spent a good two hours sitting on the floor next to the dog's cage. He'd told the girl Thumper would be fine, and he'd meant it. But considering how malnourished the poor thing was, Garrett wanted to make sure his vitals were hanging in there. So, he'd ended up cooling his butt on the same tile he'd cleaned as a teenager, holding a one-sided conversation with a half-starved, half-crippled dog about the mysterious woman he'd just seduced—or who'd seduced him. Frankly, he still wasn't clear on that part.

Time to check on the dog again. He padded on bare feet into the kennel. At first, his hazy mind couldn't grasp what was wrong with the picture. The old *Sesame Street* routine—*one of these things doesn't belong*—wandered through his head as he noticed the three hundred-dollar bills on the blanket where a dog should be.

That empty cage hit him even harder than waking up without her next to him. In the back of his mind, he'd known she would never leave town without Thumper. He'd clung to the possibility of a long recuperation and lots of doggie rehab. Seems his mystery girl had other ideas.

He sighed. She could be anywhere by now.

And he'd never even learned her name.

ICE CREAM. It might still be morning, but after spending over an hour helping a limping Thumper around the side of the house, through the garden, and into her room, Rachel deserved some ice cream. For that matter, she seriously doubted her ability to get through this morning without it.

She also needed to call Paris—if there ever was a

morning when she needed her best friend this was it—
but if she called before ten, Paris would probably dis-
own her. For now, she'd concentrate on the ice cream.

With Thumper settled on the colorful rag rug by the
bed, Rachel burrowed back against the overstuffed pillows in the Laura Ashley-fied room. She picked up the
phone and dialed the front desk.

"Chocolate, vanilla, or strawberry?" Mrs. Kelley
asked after Rachel explained why she was calling. To the
woman's credit, she didn't even comment on Rachel's
choice of breakfast fare.

"Any chance you've got Ben & Jerry's?" Rachel asked,
knowing that in a town like Braemer she should count
herself lucky just to find a national brand.

A brief pause, then, "I'll give you a pint out of my private stock. I may have moved to the country, but that
doesn't mean I'm uncivilized."

Probably should have expected that. So far this trip
had been overflowing with surprises.

She met Mrs. Kelley in the hall, then settled back in the
bed, a pint of Chunky Monkey on the table and her cell
phone against her ear. While she waited for Paris to answer, she shoveled a spoon full of frozen heaven into her
mouth and idly wondered if Ben and Jerry were up for
sainthood.

"Hey, it's me," she said when Paris answered.

"It's barely morning," Paris complained.

"It's ten." Not quite, but maybe Paris wouldn't notice.

"Like I said. So, you wanna tell me why I'm awake?"

"I think Carl seduced me last night," Rachel blurted
out before she could talk herself out of telling Paris.

A low whistle, then, "Carl MacLean? Wow. I thought
you couldn't stand him." Paris paused. "Wait a sec. You

think? Weren't you there?" Her friend sounded both amused and wary.

Rachel took another bite, postponing her answer. Cool and delicious, spoonful number two began to melt on her tongue. Only one more bite, then the trash. Even on such an unbelievable morning she wouldn't waver from her steadfast no-binging rule. "What I meant was, I'm not sure if it was me or Carl doing the seducing."

"Was it...okay?"

"Oh, yeah," she said. Her skin tingled from the memory of the way he'd stroked and kissed her, exploring her secret places with his tongue. She sighed. "It was light years beyond okay."

"Then either way you should feel better, right? I mean, he obviously thinks you're not the same girl you were in school. And you seem to have recovered from your Carl-is-the-devil-incarnate attitude. Maybe this is the start of a beautiful relationship. Should I call and warn the reunion committee? Save my bridal magazines?"

"I wouldn't start planning a shower just yet, thank you very much." The wave of guilt returned. For years, Paris had been suggesting that Rachel come back to Braemer and let everyone see how she'd changed. That was all well and good, but Rachel seriously doubted that she and Paris had had the same sort of homecoming in mind. "The fact is," she admitted, "he doesn't know it was me."

Paris said nothing.

Rachel took her last permissible bite of ice cream, swallowed, and tossed the pint into the trash. Still the line remained silent. Rachel frowned. Either Paris was in shock or she was rolling on the floor with laughter.

Rachel felt her face warm. What had seemed like a

great idea in the middle of the night was now beginning to look like a giant, mind-numbing mistake. But then, why wouldn't a naked, sweaty, erotic encounter with a gorgeous man seem like a good idea at the time? She should know better than to lay odds on what the next morning might bring.

"Oh...that's...priceless," Paris finally spit out, laughing loudly between words. "Only you could have a one-night stand with a guy you've known since kindergarten and him not have any idea who you are."

Rachel pounded the back of her head against the padded headboard. "How do I get myself into these messes?"

"Maybe this is your punishment for dating every guy in New York without a wife, a record, or an automatic weapon."

"Thanks, kid. I knew I could count on you to be a pillar of support."

"Sorry," Paris said after a few false starts. "But you have to admit it's a hoot. You have this whole persona going. Men practically line up to drool over you, but you never just jump in the sack. Then when you do, you forget to introduce yourself."

Paris started laughing again, and Rachel frowned at the phone. "I wouldn't laugh too much. You had some pretty unique man troubles not so very long ago."

Her friend's laughter faded. "I wouldn't call Devin trouble. Not exactly."

"Not anymore," Rachel admitted. "But at first he really rocked your world." She smiled, remembering last summer. Paris had been doing just fine secretly writing espionage novels under the decidedly male pseudonym of Montgomery Alexander. But the whole thing had blown up when Devin O'Malley had appeared out of nowhere and assumed Alexander's identity.

"Maybe," Paris said, "but in the end, I got a fabulous husband and a brand-new book deal."

Rachel frowned. "True. But I still don't think you should be handing out lectures on the proper way to handle men."

"Well, I'll buy that. So who does he think you are?"

Rachel shrugged. Who indeed? Then she remembered Paris couldn't see her. "Nobody, I guess. At first I wouldn't tell him my name, and then I left before he could ask again." She smiled, picturing Carl's naked hard body curled up on the couch.

"Well," Paris finally said, "who knew Braemer would've turned into such a den of iniquity?"

"Thank you. Your help in my moment of crisis has been overwhelming."

"What crisis? You've already slept with the man. Just let him know who you are and take it from there."

Tell him. That's what she had to do. Tell him and let him simmer in the knowledge that Belinda Rachel Dean had pushed him to the brink last night. *And, so sorry, bub, but you're not getting any more of that.*

Such sweet punishment, right? Sure, if she was trying to punish herself. She ran her hands over her breasts and down her stomach, quivering with the memory of his touch, his tongue. She stifled a sigh.

"Rachel?" Concern laced Paris's voice. "What am I missing?"

"Nothing. Really." Rachel sat up straighter, as if good posture would lessen the lie. But Paris knew her too well. They'd been friends forever, and now Rachel was Paris's attorney and literary agent. Secrets were hard with that kind of history.

But the whole situation was way too complicated, and she couldn't explain to Paris without confessing her true purpose in coming back to Braemer, and that wasn't something Rachel wanted to share right now. So she punted, changing the subject to Paris and Devin's upcoming book tour and other business stuff.

By the time she said goodbye and hung up, she knew she must have dug herself in deep if she didn't even want Paris knowing her scheme. Muttering a curse, she rolled onto her stomach and hung her head over the bed.

"What would you do, boy?" Rachel scratched Thumper's ears, and he raised his head, his mouth open, little canine sounds coming from his throat. Acute signs of doggie ecstacy. "You'd go for it, huh? I don't know...."

She dragged an idle finger along his coat. Last night had been a mistake. An enjoyable mistake, true. But a mistake nonetheless. Now she had a couple of problems—what to do about Carl and what to do about her plan.

There was no doubt in her mind that Carl wanted to see her again. At least he wanted to see the sultry vixen that he'd spent the night with. Truth be told, Rachel wanted nothing more than a repeat performance herself. Her passion with him had been so genuine. She'd wanted, needed him inside her, stroking her and filling her up, more than she'd ever needed anything.

She felt like Eve. She'd tasted the apple, and now she wanted the whole damn pie.

But she couldn't have it. This was Carl she was thinking about. A man who probably once spent his evenings thinking of unique ways to torment and humiliate her.

Even if he'd changed, so what? He wanted the woman from last night. Seductress Rachel.

She could be that woman for a while, but sooner or later, Carl would discover plain ol' Belinda Rachel, who'd been play-acting at success and self-confidence for the past ten years.

And Belinda Rachel wasn't the woman Carl wanted. She wasn't a woman *anybody* wanted.

No, the only thing left to do was to cross Carl off her list completely, prove her point with Jason and Derek, and head back to New York. After all, her plan wasn't a carved-in-stone, typed-in-triplicate, can't-go-with-the-flow kind of plan. Just because she'd originally wanted Carl to be Victim Number One didn't mean she couldn't now erase him entirely from the picture. There were two other fish in the sea needing a taste of Rachel-lust.

Besides, in a way, she'd already won. There was no question after last night that she'd infected Carl with a severe case of raging hormones. A few of the more choice moments from the evening jumped to mind, and she smiled. *No question at all.*

She just hadn't planned on the backlash, hadn't anticipated that one night with Carl would leave her body screaming for more. Hadn't anticipated his sweet words, his gentle manner, the way her heart swelled just looking at him. Even that stupid cowlick drove her wild.

Frowning, she bit her lip. She couldn't be interested in Carl. Not really. Just in finishing what they started. Right? Sure. That's all it was. Not real, true passion.

Damn her for not keeping condoms in her purse. They could have done the deed and now she'd be over him. Done, kaput. Out of sight, out of mind, and all that.

Instead, she was the one panting after him.

So much for planning things out.

Well, she could get back on track easily enough. Even

in a town as small as Braemer, she could avoid him. That would be no problem at all.

She rubbed Thumper's head. "Don't you think? I'll just blow him off. And after I'm gone, word'll get back to him that his mystery woman from last night was none other than little ol' me. Bingo. I win."

Thumper blinked and stretched his neck out, and Rachel took that as agreement.

Her stomach rumbled and she cast a glance toward the mostly-full pint of ice cream now melting in the garbage. "You hungry, boy? I'm starving."

A bowl of potpourri topped the dressing table. She dumped the dried flowers into the trash, wiped out the bowl, then poured some doggie chow out for Thumper. "I'm gonna go find some real food. When I get back, we'll figure out how to walk you without anyone noticing." Plus, she needed to think of a way to convince Mrs. Kelley not to make up her room every day.

She switched out of the scrubs for a pair of jeans and an oversized T-shirt, then gathered her hair back into a sloppy ponytail. The look wouldn't catch on at *Vogue* anytime soon, but since none of her victims would be hanging around a bed-and-breakfast, she figured the outfit would do.

Humming the only lines she knew from *New York, New York,* she pulled open the door and stepped into the hallway. An overabundance of small oil paintings decorated the walls, and she stifled a grin. Who knew there were so many different ways to paint a field of bluebonnets?

Midway down the hall, she paused. Mrs. Kelley's voice drifted back from the front of the old house.

"Carl MacLean, you just sit yourself right down. You

haven't stopped by for breakfast in I don't know how long."

Rachel's heart galloped and a roar filled her ears. Had he figured out where she was staying?

She considered running back to her room for decent clothes and makeup, but curiosity won out. First she'd see him, then she'd run back to her room. By the time he knocked on her door, she'd be primped and ready. And looking a hell of a lot better than she had last night.

Trying to keep the floor from creaking, she inched forward, her back to the wall. When she got to the entryway, she eased along the reception counter toward the door to the dining room, then popped her head around the door frame for a quick look.

She gasped. There, sipping coffee at a corner table, sat none other than the real Victim Number One.

Her mouth dried, and the ice cream formed a cold, hard lump in her stomach.

Oh, God. Carl MacLean. Right there in front of her.

She'd have known him anywhere.

Which left one huge, overwhelming question—if that was Carl MacLean, who had she slept with last night?

5

RACHEL JERKED HERSELF back into the hallway, out of Carl's line of sight. Oh, God, how could this have happened? How could she have made such a mistake?

He'd lied to her. The man she'd spent the past few hours craving, the man who'd caused her to rethink her entire scheme. He'd actually lied to her. Maybe not in so many words, but certainly by omission. If nothing else, the polite thing would have been for him to tell her he wasn't Carl before she'd kissed him, before she'd taken off her clothes.

And certainly before she'd exposed a piece of her heart.

She leaned back against the wall, needing its support almost as much as she needed to take a moment and get her bearings.

Carl was in the dining room drinking coffee. And he wasn't the Carl she'd slept with last night.

Even after repeating the words in her head, she still couldn't believe the huge, walloping, lotteries-have-better-odds kind of mistake she'd just made. She needed to sit down and work this out, sort through this new problem. Too bad her feet weren't keen on carrying her back to her room. Sinking through the floorboards seemed a much better choice.

An older man carrying a serious-looking wrench and wearing paint-splattered coveralls stepped into the room. He waggled the wrench in her direction. "Goin' in to breakfast, missie?"

Rachel shook her head, foolishly afraid that if she said a word she'd magically summon the real Carl from the dining area.

"That you, Roger?" Mrs. Kelley's voice drifted into the reception hall.

"Yup. Got me a youngster here who looks like a shy one. Don't seem to want to come join us for biscuits and gravy."

Say something. Rachel opened her mouth, but couldn't form words. Mortification had struck her dumb. Yes, indeed, she was well and truly back in Braemer. Good ol' tongue-tied Belinda had the floor and New York Rachel was nowhere to be seen. Probably off shopping somewhere.

Mrs. Kelley poked her head around the door frame, saw Rachel, and smiled. Rachel held her breath, sure that Carl was about to join their little soiree or that Mrs. Kelley would give her away.

To her surprise, Mrs. Kelley only winked. "Now, Roger, Rachel doesn't want to come in here."

Did she know? Rachel's stomach twisted. *How could she?*

"And she certainly doesn't want biscuits and gravy," Mrs. Kelley continued. "Don't you know anything about young women these days?"

"I reckon I know one or two things," Roger said, as Rachel debated the wisdom of just bolting down the hall and crawling under the bed.

"City girls don't eat like that. They eat healthy breakfasts with grains and fruit." She poked Roger in the gut with the end of a wooden spoon. "You should try it sometime."

"Sissy food."

Mrs. Kelley turned to Rachel and winked. "And Rachel's already had a healthy breakfast in her room. Haven't you, dear?"

Rachel nodded, remembering her three bites of Chunky Monkey. Looks like that was going to be breakfast. "Couldn't have been healthier. Thanks."

She was relieved that her mouth had started working again, but the Carl problem was still sitting in the dining room, and she needed to get back to her room before he decided to join the party. Scanning the hall, she noticed the stack of newspapers by the door. "Actually, I just came out for a paper." She crossed the polished floor and tucked an anorexic copy of the *Braemer Bee* under her arm. "Gotta keep up with the world news."

With a wave and what she hoped was a chipper smile, she headed back toward her room, Roger's final comment—"But she's such a scrawny thing"—ringing in her ears.

The second she closed her door, Thumper's tail started beating a rhythm. She dropped to the floor and stretched out on the rag rug next to him, her fingers idly stroking the short, silky fur. "So what should I do, buddy?"

He whined, then yawned.

"Sorry if my dilemma bores you." She rolled onto her back and scooted up next to him. Thumper snuffled at her ear, then settled back into his nap. Rachel stared at the tin tiles lining the ceiling, trying to read their pattern like a psychic reading Tarot cards. Nothing. If the old house held any secrets, it wasn't giving them up for her.

In the past few minutes, her perception of the world had been thrown seriously out of whack. Last night, she'd thought she was the one in control, the one doing the seducing. This morning, whatever victory she could claim had been blown to smithereens. For one thing, she'd awakened with the uncomfortable realization that she still needed him, hungered for him. Whoever *him* was. Which brought her to major problem number two—she'd seduced the wrong guy. So *victory* was probably overstating her case.

Stretched out on the floor, she closed her eyes, willing herself to approach the situation calmly and rationally. With three years of law school under her belt, if she couldn't attack this problem one step at a time, she should return her diploma and ask for a refund.

First things first. *Carl.* The real one. What to do about him? She pulled herself up, her back resting against the bed as her fingers kneaded the soft spot at the base of Thumper's neck. Carl hadn't seen her last night or this morning. So as far as he was concerned, nothing had happened.

The thought relieved her more than she wanted to admit. She tried to tell herself it was only because Carl's newfound identity meant that her original plan was still on track. But the truth was that the man last night had touched something in her she wasn't sure she wanted to explore. Knowing it wasn't her nemesis who'd made her feel that way somehow made these new sensations a little less scary.

Frustrated, she banged her forehead against her knees. How she felt about her mystery man wasn't the point. The good news was that Carl MacLean had just been reinstated in the Victim Number One spot.

Still, if last night's victim wasn't Carl, then who exactly had she spent the night with?

Her mind drifted back to the way he'd touched her, the sweet things he'd whispered in her ear. The miraculous way he'd set her senses on edge with nothing more than the touch of his hand. Even with only the tip of his finger, he'd been able to coax her body into revealing its secrets.

Last night she'd shared passion with a man who'd stirred feelings in her she hadn't known existed.

And she didn't even know his name.

Whoever he was, he wasn't Carl. Instead, he'd been impersonating her nemesis. But why? To humiliate her again, after all these years? Maybe this was another big prank, and on the night of the reunion dance it would be Rachel—not the Stooges—standing front and center. One of the Stooges would call into the microphone "Will the real Carl MacLean please stand up?" while all her classmates laughed and jeered, just like they'd done ten years ago.

No. He'd been kind last night. Gentle. He'd touched her heart.

He'd lied to her.

With a mental shove, she pushed the thought away. Maybe he had, but she didn't want to believe it. And she hadn't exactly been a fount of honesty, either.

She got up and paced the room, back and forth across the hardwood floor from the bathroom to the French doors that opened onto the garden. She stopped and looked down at Thumper, his eyes closed and his nose twitching, chasing cats in a doggie dream. "He was a real vet," she whispered. "He wasn't lying about that. And he sure fixed you up fine."

Running her fingers through her hair, she went over what she knew. He'd been driving a truck with vet journals addressed to Carl MacLean. When she'd called him Dr. MacLean, he'd answered. He'd had keys to the animal clinic, and he'd fixed up Thumper.

But had she ever called him Carl?

Come to think of it, she didn't think so.

Maybe he didn't realize what she thought. Yeah, right. And maybe she was an out-of-work chorus girl. Of course he realized. And he hadn't said one damn word.

So who was her mystery vet who looked so much like Carl? His uncle? Cousin? Hell, he could even be Carl's brother. She'd never even known him, just met him briefly the time Dr. MacLean had fixed up Dexter. Of course, she'd heard all the gossip about how he and his father didn't get along. From the sound of it, she'd never expect the eldest MacLean to come riding back into Braemer.

But, people did mend fences.

She licked her lips and glanced at the phone. Might as well ask a few questions. Sure. Why not? Before she could talk herself out of it, she grabbed the phone off the bedside table, then punched the number for the reception desk. "Who runs that vet clinic on the county road?" she asked as soon as Mrs. Kelley answered.

"Dr. MacLean, dear. Do you need a vet?"

"No. Just curious. Carl MacLean? The younger MacLean? About thirty?"

"Oh, goodness, no. Dr. MacLean's well into his sixties. And Carl wouldn't know a pig from a pony. He's a lawyer here in town." She paused for a moment. "He's here now. Would you like me to fetch him?"

"No. No, thank you." She paused. "Does Dr. MacLean have any other children?" If Rachel was right, and they were estranged, a relative newcomer like Mrs. Kelley might not realize the old vet had another son.

"He sure does. His oldest. Garrett."

Rachel shut her eyes and exhaled. *Garrett.* Yes, she remembered now. She kept her eyes closed and clutched the handset a little tighter. "Garrett's not a vet, too, is he?"

"Well, I don't know. He lives in Los Angeles, you know."

Rachel frowned, not sure what Los Angeles had to do with being a vet. Didn't they have pets in California? Not that it mattered. If Garrett was in Los Angeles, he certainly hadn't seduced her in the clinic last night. "Well, thanks anyway, Mrs. Kelley. I'll just—"

"Would you like me to ask him?"

Her heart skipped a beat. "I...I'm.... Excuse me?"

"Or you can ask him yourself," Mrs. Kelley added, as Rachel held her breath, terrified of where the conversation was headed. "He's staying in the room right above yours."

GARRETT COULDN'T BELIEVE his luck. Unless he was mistaken, the dark green sedan parked under Mrs. Kelley's oak tree meant that his runaway temptress was staying at the same B-and-B he'd checked into yesterday afternoon. He grinned. If he couldn't manage to get close to her while they were both sleeping under the same roof, then he had no business calling himself a red-blooded American male.

Inside, he marched across the reception area, his eyes scanning the room. He paused at the threshold to the dining area, taking in each table, making sure she wasn't sipping coffee or eating a biscuit. He glanced toward Carl, who waved him over. Garrett acknowledged his brother with a nod, but stayed still as he continued his search of the room. Mrs. Kelley's handyman sat at one table, a couple of biscuits floating in gravy on a plate in front of him. A young couple held hands in a corner, oblivious to everything but each other. A balding man with a few strands of hair combed sideways over his head sat by the window reading a paper.

But his mystery date was nowhere to be found.

He exhaled, realizing he was actually relieved. For some reason she'd wanted only one night with him—with Carl, actually. And she'd walked out without even saying goodbye. So if he intended to win her over—if he wanted to finish what they'd started—then he needed a plan. Needed the upper hand. And his first step was finding out her name.

Carl looked up as Garrett approached. "Hey, big brother."

Garrett barely even slowed down. "Give me a second," he said, heading for the kitchen in search of Mrs. Kelley. He found her squatting in front of the open oven, sliding in a cookie sheet.

He offered a hand to help her to her feet. "Do you have a young woman staying here? Dark hair, pretty, about so high," he asked, using his hand to slice the air near his nose. "Has a black Lab with her."

"Well, except for the dog, I'd say Rachel fits that description."

Garrett cocked his head. "Rachel?" He rolled the name around in his mind. *Rachel.* It suited her.

"Rachel Dean," Mrs. Kelley added. The name had a familiar ring, but Garrett couldn't place it. Mrs. Kelley's brow furrowed. "She was asking about you, too. You and Carl."

He held his breath, trying to look nonchalant, but his heart beat faster just from knowing he'd stayed in her thoughts. "Oh?"

"Asked if Carl was a vet, then asked the same thing about you. I told her Carl was no vet, but I didn't know about you." She paused, giving him a chance to reveal his profession. When he kept silent, she looked away, clearing her throat. "Why'd you think she had a dog?"

"Long story," he said, trying to figure out what Rachel could have done with Thumper.

Skirting a butcher-block island, she headed for the refrigerator. She pulled it open and peered inside. "I adore puppies. It's a shame I can't let the little darlings stay, but they're a bit rough on the furniture."

He nodded, suddenly sure that Rachel had smuggled Thumper into her room. He fought a grin, wondering if, during her impulsive act of taking the dog with her, she'd remembered that she'd have to feed and walk it. At least he knew where to find Thumper. Hopefully he'd be back on track with Rachel tomorrow, but even if he wasn't, he'd figure out a way to get in her room to check the dog's bandages and give him another dose of antibiotics.

Two problems down, one to go. Hey, he was on a roll.

Mrs. Kelley grabbed a gallon of milk and tucked a carton of eggs in the crook of her arm. "Shall I mention you asked about her?" After setting the food on the counter, she reached toward the pot rack suspended from the ceiling.

Garrett shook his head. "No, thanks." He stepped past the kitchen's butcher-block island and pulled down the mixing bowl she was reaching for. "I'll handle it."

Mrs. Kelley smiled. "Then it's a budding romance I've got brewing in my house, is it? Perhaps you're the gentleman she was mooning over this morning."

Mooning? "Pardon me?"

The older woman tapped herself on the head with her index finger. "Women's intuition. Plus, I've been around the block a time or two." She glanced toward the kitchen door and back to Garrett. "Not that I'm gossiping, mind you. But when a woman has ice cream for breakfast, there's only one explanation. Man troubles." She winked at him. "And it looks like you may be the man in question." She paused, her eyes narrowing slightly. "Especially considering that neither one of you made it to your rooms last night."

Garrett frowned, suddenly feeling as uncomfortable as a teenager caught breaking curfew. Then her words sank in.

Ice cream.

That meant Mrs. Kelley was probably right. He'd dated enough women in his life to know that if Rachel was resorting to early morning comfort food it could only mean one thing—she was as confused about what had happened between them as he was.

Thank God he wasn't the only one.

"Mrs. Kelley, you're a dear." He planted a quick kiss on her cheek, then headed toward the dining room, pleased that his day seemed to be coming together. The scenario he'd faced this morning had seemed insurmountable. She'd left without saying goodbye. She'd believed he was Carl. And he hadn't known her name or how to find her.

But what had started out as a disaster, had suddenly become salvageable. In only a few hours, he'd found out that they were sharing a house, and that she knew he wasn't Carl. And, most important, he'd also learned her real name.

Of course, the situation still wasn't sunshine and roses. For one thing, ice cream or not, he had no real sign that she wanted to see him again. She hadn't left him a message begging him to come to her room and pick up where they'd left off. Nor had she tried to phone him or even asked Mrs. Kelley to tell him she was here. None of which boded well for his hope that she was naked under the covers, longing to see him again.

But on the other hand, Mrs. Kelley had said she was infatuated with a man. So much so that she'd eaten ice cream for breakfast. And unless he was sorely mistaken, he was that man. It wasn't much, but it was something. And at this stage of the game, Garrett was happy to claim whatever triumphs he could.

Feeling a little more in control of the Rachel situation, he went back into the dining room to join Carl. Since he was on a roll, now seemed as good a time as any to press his brother to explain his reason for not going to the re-union dance.

GARRETT TOOK ANOTHER SIP of coffee and watched Carl slide scrambled eggs around on his plate with a fork. Carl hadn't wanted to talk about the Belinda girl, but after Garrett insisted, Carl had nodded, then started drawing patterns in his food. Garrett waited, knowing that Carl wasn't stalling, just collecting his thoughts.

"Up until high school, everyone pretty much ignored her," Carl finally said. "She was smart. Straight A's. But she was one of those invisible kids."

"Were you mean to her?" Garrett asked, not sure he could picture Carl going out of his way to hurt anybody, even with the force of peer pressure pushing him on.

"Me, personally?" Carl asked, then went on without waiting for an answer. "I suppose. But no more than everyone else. I'd made varsity my freshman year and was trying to fit in. They'd call out names like Roly-Poly and Four Eyes when she walked by. I never joined in, but I never tried to stop them either."

He picked up his coffee cup, but didn't take a sip. A muscle jerked in his cheek, and he looked away, keeping his eyes wide as he focused on the ceiling. "The thing is, I laughed, too. You know?" He looked at Garrett, his brow furrowed, real pain in his eyes. "I knew it wasn't funny, but I laughed, too."

Garrett's chest tightened, feeling the humiliation this girl must have suffered, and also the remorse his kid brother now felt. "You're right, you behaved badly. But you were a kid, and it was a long time ago."

"It wasn't the whole school, of course," Carl said, picking at a biscuit. "I mean, some folks were okay. But the kids I hung with were brutal. She was poor, so that made it worse, and she didn't have a dad—he'd run off with some stripper years before. For some reason Jason really focused on her. He'd write things about her in the bathroom, call her names. Basically, he just wouldn't leave her alone. And Derek was right there with him."

Garrett bit back on his growing disgust. He didn't give a damn what Jason Stilwell had done. The boy had been a rich, spoiled prick, and he was sure the adult Jason was just as bad. He forced the twenty-thousand dollar question out from behind clenched teeth. "What did you do?"

Carl laughed. One short, sardonic burst that managed to convey infinite self-disgust. "Not a damn thing. At least not then. I erased what I could from the bathroom walls, but that's about it. By that time, Jason and Derek and I were the team's golden boys. If we kept it up, I knew they'd be handing me football scholarships on silver platters. So I didn't want to piss off Jason or Derek. They could make me look bad on the field. And I wanted a football scholarship."

"Well, you got the scholarship all right." He tried to keep his voice level, but couldn't completely hide his disappointment. Carl had always been a decent kid. But he'd been coddled and pampered—by Garrett as much as by anyone. "I guess that means you three kept teasing this poor girl for your entire senior year?"

Carl shook his head. "No. When they started up again senior year, I couldn't take it anymore."

Garrett relaxed, relieved to hear his brother had finally grown a backbone.

"She'd taken the SAT early and her score made school history," Carl continued. "Then the rumor was she'd applied for early admission to some Ivy League school and got in. Plus, she wrote some essay that won a statewide contest. So despite everything, I figured this was one determined kid. Determined, but lonely. I never saw her talk to anyone in the halls. Most of the time she sat by herself at lunch."

Carl shrugged. "I figured she needed a friend," he said, then laughed. "*That* was a major project. Getting her to trust me, I mean."

Considering what Carl had told him, Garrett could certainly see why. "But she did?"

"Eventually. And I found out she was really nice. Bookish, but nice." He wiped bits of biscuit off his hands with his napkin. "Not that we became best buddies or anything, but we'd talk between classes and I walked her home a couple of times."

So far, so good. But Garrett knew the story didn't end well. And he had a feeling he knew why. "Jason and Derek, right?"

Carl nodded. "They pretty much screwed up every thing."

"How?"

"By doing the same thing I was doing. And more. Hell, they even roughed up some guys that were giving Belinda a hard time. And I was so dense I thought they meant it. I thought they'd really come around." He picked the fork back up and moved the eggs around some more. "When my girlfriend broke up with me, I figured what the heck? So I asked Belinda to the prom. I figured we'd go as friends, and she'd get a kick out of it."

"What happened?" Garrett asked, his fingers itching for a cigarette. Instead, he clenched and unclenched his fists, certain he already knew the answer.

"Jason said my plan was genius. String her along until the prom and then—boom." He pounded the table. "Slimy worm. I told him no way. She was my date and that's just the way it was."

His words spilled out, tumbling over themselves, anger and shame permeating in his voice. "That's when he told me they had something special planned for her. Like I said, Jason had really fixated on her. I don't know why. But I told him to go to hell, and he told me that he'd see to it my football scholarship was revoked."

"You were three days from graduation. How was he going to manage that?"

Carl laughed, an ugly, bitter sound. "That's what I said. And he very casually reminded me that most football teams weren't interested in players with broken ribs and kneecaps." He shrugged. "So I caved. I walked her right into Jason's claws and saw him humiliate her in front of the entire class."

"So you're not going to the dance because you don't want to see her?" He spit out the words. "That seems like the chicken's way out, little brother."

Carl shook his head, eyes wide. "God, no," he insisted. "If I thought she'd show, I'd be there in a heartbeat. I'd at least go and apologize." He looked deep into Garrett's eyes. "I promise you that." He exhaled loudly and shook his head. "But I don't see her rolling back into town for this reunion. Why would she? Not after the way we treated her. No, the reason I'm not going is 'cause I feel like a heel. I was a complete jerk, and I'm not real keen on spending a weekend surrounded by pictures of me winning the big game and other pathetic little memories. Not when I've got something like this on my conscience."

"Why don't you look her up? Apologize? Explain what happened at the prom?"

Carl shrugged. "I thought about it. But what if she's put it behind her? On top of everything else, I don't want to be the one to rip open a wound that's already healed."

Carl's reasoning made some sense. The girl had probably moved on, had a nice life, two point five kids, and never even gave Carl a passing thought. Garrett certainly hoped so. After the crappy way Carl had treated her, she deserved a happy ending. His stomach rolled, his anger and disappointment with Carl settling in his gut like indigestion.

"Poor Belinda," he said, feeling almost like he knew the girl, wishing he could help.

Something Carl mentioned yesterday tugged at his memory, and he looked at his brother through narrowed eyes. "What was her full name again?"

"Belinda Dean," Carl said, his words hitting Garrett with more force than a sucker punch. "Belinda Rachel Dean."

Rachel. *His* Rachel. Coherent thought fled as fury consumed him. All he knew was that his world was spinning out of orbit and that Carl had hurt Rachel.

His fingers curled, tighter and tighter, and the next thing Garrett knew he was standing up, his hand throbbing, and Carl was splayed out on the floor.

Rubbing his jaw, Carl looked up at him. "What the hell was that for?"

"Belinda," he said, forcing the word out. "It was for Belinda."

6

WITHOUT RACHEL, the clinic that had seemed romantic by night now seemed empty and antiseptic. Garrett wandered through the reception area and into the break room, eyeing their couch, his body tightening with the memory of her touch.

Damn Carl.

It had taken every last ounce of his willpower not to rush out of the dining room, find Rachel, and pull her into his arms.

To Carl's credit, he'd almost jumped out of his chair when Garrett told him he'd seen Rachel in town, he was so eager to find her. Of course, Garrett didn't mention just how much of her he'd seen. Under the circumstances, a little prudence went a long way.

Carl had insisted on tracking the girl down and launching into an apology. But Garrett convinced him to stay away for now. At least until he worked out the little problem with his identity. And he needed to solve that as quickly as possible, because Garrett wanted to hold her, protect her, help her forget every hurt that Jason, Derek and Carl had laid at her feet. And he couldn't do that until they'd cleared the air.

In reality, he barely knew her, but needed to make a difference. He told himself it was just guilt by association—his brother had been an ass, so Garrett wanted to make it better. But the truth was, his need went so much deeper. Until he'd met Rachel, he hadn't realized just how lonely he'd been these past years. She'd touched something in him, and now he wanted to make the world right for her.

In the end, he forced himself to leave and go to the clinic because she surely needed time to mull over last night. From what Mrs. Kelley said, Rachel must've figured out he wasn't Carl. Common sense suggested that until she'd had a little time to get used to the idea, he shouldn't be within throwing distance of her.

Frowning, he popped the lid off Blinky's food canister and scooped some cat food into her bowl. The resident cat came running, and he idly scratched her head as she chowed down. "She's probably pretty pissed at me, don't you think?"

"Who?"

The question clearly hadn't come from the cat, so Garrett spun around to gape at Jennie. "Dammit, Jenn, don't you knock?" She'd scared him to death, but he couldn't help but smile. He'd missed his stepmother something fierce.

She dangled a key. "It's Sunday and your dad and I own the place. Why would I knock?"

He nodded, surprised by a tug of melancholy. In front of Carl, he'd called the clinic "podunk." But it wasn't. Not really. For about half his life, this clinic had been his focal point. He'd started out cleaning cages in grade school, and by high school, had moved up to doing most everything short of surgery. Carl, Jr. may have been the Wonder Child outside those doors, but in here, their father had actually paid attention to Garrett. It might not have been warm and fuzzy, but it had been something.

That fact had made the hurt run so much deeper when his dad had kept silent, letting Garrett run off to college and vet school in California without even hinting that maybe he should come back and pitch in at the MacLean Animal Hospital.

Jennie pulled a soda out of the fridge, then faced him, her eyes crinkling as she smiled. "So, who's pissed at you?"

With a wave, he brushed the question aside. "Nobody." Even after all these years, he couldn't rat on his baby brother, and there was no way to explain this soap opera without mentioning Carl and Rachel and high school and the whole damn fiasco.

"Everybody loves me," he added. "Or hadn't you heard?"

Her face tightened and he immediately regretted the words. He'd meant the comment as a throwaway, but he was sure Jennie heard it as a criticism of his dad. "I didn't mean—"

"I know." She glanced around. "Why are you here?"

He moved to the couch while she settled into the chair. "In Texas? Or at the clinic?"

"I know why you came back home." She leaned over to stroke Blinky. "I mean here, today. Did you forget that I'd come by? Or did you want to talk?"

He had to chuckle. There might be a bit more gray on her head and a few more lines on her face, but she was still the same perceptive Jennie who always knew when something was on his mind. "I wouldn't even know where to start."

"Is she from Braemer?"

"She?"

Jennie grinned. "Keep up with the conversation, Garrett. The woman who's pissed."

"Right." He fought a chuckle. "No," he added, then frowned, wondering where Rachel did live. Once again, he was struck by how little he knew about her. Remarkable, considering how much she'd already permeated his life. Well, that was a deficiency he intended to correct just as soon as he could.

"That's a shame."

"Why? I live in California, remember?"

Jennie shrugged. "I can still hope, can't I?"

He squinted at her. "Hope what?"

She looked at him like he was dense. "That you'll stay, of course. We miss you. If you had a girlfriend here..."

"We haven't exactly ventured into relationship territory," he said. "I'd be happy to go there, but we're not there yet."

"Well, where are you?"

He ignored the question, pretty sure that Jennie wouldn't understand the dynamics of a relationship that kicked off with phenomenal anonymous sex, and not certain he understood himself.

"Besides," he continued, "I'm not sure that I'd stay even if she lived here." He wanted that to be absolutely clear, half afraid that if he didn't keep reality firmly in mind, he'd simply give in and follow her to the ends of the earth. And that would be mind-bogglingly stupid.

Garrett's practice outside L.A. was thriving, so it would be financial suicide to pack up and come to Texas. Besides, no matter what Carl said, his dad didn't want him here. Setting up shop as a country vet just wasn't in the cards. "I'm just here to help," he added, needing to convince Jenn and himself.

Her face tightened and she shoved up from the chair. "I'm going to walk through the kennel. You stay as long as you want."

Huh? His head swam. He had no idea what he'd done, but somehow he'd managed to tick her off. Not an easy feat, since she was about the most mild-mannered person on the planet.

He stopped her in the doorway. "Jenn? What am I missing?"

"I just expected more from you, Garrett." She looked toward the floor. "I know your father hurt you. I'm not blind. I just thought you were a bigger man, that's all."

Clearly they weren't on the same page. "I don't know what the hell you're talking about." He tried to keep the frustration out of his voice, but failed.

When she looked up at him, hurt shone in her eyes. "It took a lot of courage for your father to admit he needs your help."

His throat went dry as a knot formed in his stomach. Had she really said that?

Jennie sighed. "I never expected you'd just pack up and move home, but I thought you'd at least consider staying on for a few months." She smoothed her flowerprint skirt. "You've got a staff out there, but your father's got no help at all."

"Dad wanted me to come?" His voice sounded far away, like someone else was speaking.

"Isn't that why you're here?"

"I came for Carl. It wasn't until I hit Braemer that he told me Dad wanted me here." He laughed, short and bitter. "And I didn't believe him."

"Your father's getting on. He's thinking about his family—his mistakes." She kissed him on the cheek. "See if you can't cut him some slack."

Garrett nodded wordlessly as his reality shifted. Everything he'd known, everything he'd believed, had changed in the blink of an eye. If what Jenn and Carl said was true, his dad actually admitted needing his help. He kept repeating the thought, his mind trying to grasp this new reality, so different from the texture and color of his life growing up.

Taking a deep breath, he smiled. He'd barely set foot back in Braemer and already he'd had an overture of peace from his father and a mind-altering encounter with an anonymous temptress.

If this kept up, the next twenty-four hours promised to be damned interesting.

THE COTTON GIN hadn't changed at all. Paris's father had brought the girls there once during one of his political fund-raisers. They'd been about eight, and Mr. Sommers had been running for county judge. All Rachel remembered was the live music, locking hands with Paris, and spinning on the dance floor while the band blared out the Cotton-Eye Joe. She sighed. Until Paris had moved away, Braemer had actually been bearable.

From the doorway, she scoped out the cavernous room. Peanut shells littered the floor. Long folding tables topped with red-and-white checkered tablecloths lined the inside perimeter of the room on three walls, leaving one wall free for a band that was setting up on a raised wooden platform. A bar that served only beer was tucked into one corner, a crowd nearly blocking the neon sign from view. Another bar, this one with jug wine and coolers, filled the other corner.

It had taken her the whole day to get up the nerve to come out tonight. Except for sneaking Thumper into the garden during the late afternoon, she'd spent the day locked in her room, Thumper beside her, afraid that if she stepped outside, she'd see Garrett. And she wasn't sure she was ready to see him yet.

The truth was, part of her still wanted to be in that room, snuggled under the covers and catching up on her reading. She'd almost stayed, but she'd forced herself to get up and get dressed. If she ignored her plan and cowered in her room, then Jason and Derek and Carl would have already won this round—and they didn't even know they were playing.

So here she was, hanging out in a dance hall, country music blaring out of a jukebox, wearing Ann Taylor jeans instead of Levi's, finely stitched Italian boots since she didn't own Ropers, and a white Liz Claiborne T-shirt. Sort of the Fifth Avenue version of country.

She dropped into one of the metal folding chairs and crossed her legs, schooling her face into an expression of polite interest. Her fingers drummed the tabletop as she scanned the room looking for Carl. This used to be his favorite hangout. Even on a Sunday night, it was still a local hot spot. And here she was, back on track. Maybe she'd been temporarily derailed by one of the MacLean boys, but when Carl showed up tonight, Rachel intended to jump-start her plan.

"Hey, baby," hollered a drunk bubba directly in her ear. "How about you and me get a little private two-step going?"

She stood up, flashing her most confident smile. *This* kind of scene she could handle in her sleep. "Why don't you go sober up, sugar?" she said, patting him on the cheek. She noticed the ring on his left hand and glanced down pointedly. "Besides, isn't your dance card pretty much filled?"

Leaving Bubba in her wake, she headed for the bar, actually grateful for the man's attention, however misguided. She was in Braemer, and she looked hot. Her. Rachel. She glanced around the room, noticing the interested stares from nearby men. Belinda Rachel might have made an appearance or two in the past twenty-four hours, but right now she'd been firmly banished from the floor. Rachel had the situation well under control.

She licked her lips. Time to get moving.

With a few "excuse mes" and a couple of "coming throughs", she managed to squeeze her way to the front of the beer line, suffering only one or two butt pinches in the process.

"Draft or longneck?" the bartender asked.

"Longneck," she said, then took the bottle he thrust at her. She leaned over the counter. "Listen, do you know Carl MacLean?"

The bartender filled a mug, topping it off with a nice head of foam, then handed it to a fellow standing next to Rachel. "Sure thing." He grinned at her. "You in town for the reunion?"

"Let's just say I'm trying to catch up with a few old friends." She smiled. "So, do you think Carl will come by?"

"Could be." He lifted his chin, glancing at some spot behind her. "There's his brother," the bartender said, and Rachel's chest tightened. "Why don't you ask him?"

"Thanks," she said, hoping her voice sounded normal. "Good idea." But she didn't turn around. Not yet. She needed a second to pull herself together. *Garrett was right there, somewhere behind her.* She took a breath and flexed her fingers, trying to tamp the warm glow that coursed through her body merely at the mention of his name.

Of course, she should have expected he'd show up. She'd managed to avoid him for the entire day. Murphy's Law pretty much dictated that her luck would run out.

She could handle this. Just because her entire being craved him didn't mean she would lose her focus. She was here on a mission, after all. The only MacLean that mattered was Carl. No way was she going to get involved with Garrett. He was just one more MacLean man that she couldn't trust.

And it was just physical, right? The sweet comfort that washed over her every time she thought about him, the ridiculous feeling that he could make everything better if only she'd let him—well, that was nothing but hormone-induced brain-drain. It had to be. Her heart might believe she'd stumbled into something special, but her head knew simple lust when she saw it. He'd lied to her. How special could it have been?

You lied, too.

She bit her lip, straining to focus. She'd walked into the Cotton Gin with a mission, and she was damn well going to get it back on track. And that meant chalking last night up to experience, and moving on.

"Hello, there."

She froze, his voice sliding down her spine like warm honey.

Slowly she turned around, a shudder rippling through her at the sight of him. Every intent to walk away evaporated, replaced instead with a need to lose herself in his arms. A need so intense it seemed physical, almost painful. But he was bad news—she needed to keep telling herself that. Maybe it would eventually stick.

"Hello, Garrett," she mumbled.

He smiled, and she knew with sudden certainty that she was playing out of her league. She dropped her gaze, trying to get her bearings and silently cursing herself, feeling almost ashamed that he'd so easily pierced her armor.

His low chuckle piqued her anger, and she embraced

the emotion, more comfortable clinging to calculated rage than the unpredictable feelings he'd sparked last night. This was the man who'd deceived her, after all.

A man who would never hurt you.

The thought came unbidden and she shoved it away. He'd made love to her under false pretenses. She'd done the same, true, but she'd had an agenda. He'd simply been deceitful. Not a very coherent rationalization, but it was the best she could do since her brain was turning to mush under his steady gaze.

As he took her elbow and led her to an empty table, she gnawed on her lower lip. If his smile was any indication, he wasn't aware of her annoyance.

"You want to tell me what's so funny?" she demanded.

"Just that it looks like we've both done our homework."

She squinted, not sure what he was talking about.

He held out his hand, and she took it automatically. His fingers curled around hers, warm and strong. "Probably a little late, but I'm Garrett MacLean. It's a pleasure to meet you." He grinned. "And if I'm not mistaken, you're Belinda Rachel Dean."

She gasped, not sure which had knocked her more off-kilter. The fact that he knew who she was, or the sudden realization that, no matter how hard she tried, she would always be Belinda Rachel.

No. That might be her name, but that wasn't who she was. Not anymore. She'd come back to prove it. And she might as well start now.

Slowly, she pulled her hand free of his, her self-confidence and control returning as the distance between them increased. "I prefer just plain Rachel now."

One song ended and the jukebox blared out a new

tune, an old George Strait song about oceanfront property, the volume cranked up enough to make conversation difficult. Garrett moved his chair closer until his thigh brushed hers. She tried to ignore the warmth that crept up her leg, but when he leaned closer, his breath teased her ear, and she came near to losing control.

"I don't think you're plain at all, Rachel," he whispered, his voice deep and husky, familiar in timbre and full of desire.

The man was dangerous. He did things to her heart, her head. She scooted her chair away, desperate to put some space between them. Even then, the distance taunted her. That one strip of air between their denim-clad legs seemed charged. She could practically feel the electrons buzzing and humming.

"So tell me about yourself, plain old Rachel."

She smiled despite herself. "Tell you what?"

"Well," he said, leaning in closer and hooking an arm around her shoulder, "this is sort of our second date. We should be well past the getting-to-know-you stage."

"This is not a date," she said, but somehow the brush of his forearm against her shoulder stole the conviction from her voice.

"Sure it is," he said, again moving his chair closer so that their legs touched. "You already know about me. Vet, California, brother. That pretty much sums it up."

She fought a grin and he looked at her expectantly, but she wasn't about to play this game.

"And what about plain old Rachel?" When she kept silent, he held an imaginary microphone in front of her. "Just the facts, ma'am."

At that, she really did laugh. Not only did he sound silly, making his voice deep and monotone, but he seemed so earnest about wanting to get to know her.

And she wanted him to know her; heaven help her, she really did.

He leaned in closer. "Tell me, Rachel," he said, his voice low. "Give me just a nugget. I want to know a little about the woman I made love with."

Made love. She clung to the words, wondering if he meant them. "I'm an attorney," she said, finally. "But mostly I run a literary agency. I live in Manhattan. Sort of."

"Sort of?"

"I lost the lease on my apartment right before I came here." She eyed him. "That's all you're getting. I'd say we're even."

With the side of his hand, he stroked her cheek. "See, that wasn't so hard."

Wordlessly, she nodded. He was right. Talking with Garrett was easy, *comfortable.* The thought scared her. Somewhere along the line her heart had turned west while her head was still heading north.

Something about him called to her, confused her. And now he'd managed to get under her skin without even trying. Alarm bells jangled in her head. She needed to remember why she was in Braemer. Her plan. *That* was her priority.

He'd deceived her, and she clung to that fact like a life-line. "You lied to me."

He leaned back, the corner of his mouth twitching. "I guess that means we've passed the getting-to-know-you stage."

"You lied," she repeated, just to make sure he realized she was ignoring his attempt at levity.

"Did I?"

She raised an eyebrow and the twitch turned into a smile.

"Well, I suppose technically I did," he said.

"Technically? You told me you were Carl. How is that technical?" She'd raised her voice to be heard above the jukebox, but finished her tirade as the song ended. Six or seven nearby patrons turned in their chairs and stared, probably wondering what the heck the new chick was shouting about. So much for making a kick-ass first impression. But at least no one would think she was shy.

"I never actually said I was Carl. Just that I was Dr. MacLean." He shrugged. "And I am."

She rolled her eyes. "What? Are you running for President? I don't think those kind of fine line distinctions work out here in the real world." She turned her chair so she faced him head-on. "You knew damn well I thought you were Carl, and you didn't say one word."

"You weren't exactly open about your identity either," he said, taking her hand. "Now why was that?"

"That's not the point," she said, as his fingers traced the lines of her palm, the touch both casual and erotic. She tried to ignore the heat that coursed through her body, starting from the tips of her fingers and centering between her thighs. "You weren't under any illusions about me."

She looked up at him, searching for answers in his clear blue eyes, wondering if he'd seen something more than the mask she'd shown him. "Why, Garrett?"

"I like it when you say my name." He lifted her hand to his mouth and kissed her fingertips, and she shuddered at his touch, sure that she'd lost control of the situation.

She pulled her hand away, trying to ignore the tiny part of her that hoped he *had* seen behind her mask and wanted her anyway.

"Garrett," she repeated, "why?"

For a moment, he stared at her, then stood, holding out his hand to help her up. "Dance with me and I'll tell you."

She shook her head even as she put her hand in his. "I don't think that's such a good idea."

"Just one dance. Please."

He tugged gently, and she let him ease her to her feet. One dance. She knew she shouldn't. Despite the little voice in her head telling her that this man was different, she knew better than to trust a MacLean.

But right then, right there, she wanted to be in his arms.

One dance. She'd have her answers, they'd part ways, and she'd be back on track. Surely one little dance wouldn't hurt.

But as she let him lead her to the dance floor, as his arms wrapped around her, as her pulse quickened, the soft strains of Patsy Cline's "Crazy" floated around them, and she wondered if that song wasn't somehow completely appropriate.

7

As Patsy faded out, George Strait kicked back in. "The Chair." Another slow dance. Garrett allowed himself a sigh of relief. No way was he letting this woman out of his embrace, not even to do the two-step.

They fit together perfectly, but he'd known they would. He'd discovered last night how well their bodies melded, as if she'd been created especially for him. And now that she was back in his arms, he intended to keep her there.

Her nearness teased and excited him, kicking every nerve ending in his body into overdrive. Just a slight tilt of his head and he could lose himself in her scent, could savor the soft skin at her temple. He wanted to indulge in each of her delicious, feminine places, wanted the taste of her to linger in his mouth. Stifling a moan, he let his lips graze the top of her ear and felt her stiffen.

"You're tense," he whispered.

"No, I'm not."

"Sweetheart, I can feel every inch of you." That earned him a breathy sigh. Clearly, she could feel him, too—and knew exactly how much he wanted her.

He trailed his fingers down her back, finally cupping her perfect rear with one hand. Her soft sigh washed over him, letting him know she welcomed his touch.

"Garrett..."

"We'll talk, I promise. But for now, just let me hold you."

Slowly, almost imperceptibly, she relaxed in his arms, her body molding to his. In time with the music, she trailed a finger along the back of his neck, just under his collar. The caress was so light, he wasn't sure she was even aware of what her finger was doing.

He, on the other hand, was acutely aware. Fire coursed through him, and he summoned every ounce of willpower to keep from catching her in a kiss and letting the flames consume them both. They'd already moved at the speed of light. For right now, he could take it a little slower, even though her nearness threatened to drive him crazy.

He wanted her near, needed to hold and touch and stroke her. Wanted to laugh and joke with her. Wanted to peel away each of her layers and understand the woman she'd become. No thanks to his brother, Rachel's childhood hadn't exactly been sunshine and laughter. And yet she'd grown into a determined, intelligent woman full of spunk and fire. A woman self-assured enough to initiate a seduction.

Ultimately, of course, it had been a mutual seduction, but Rachel had definitely set the ball rolling. She'd wanted to seduce him, and she'd succeeded admirably.

Not him. Carl. Garrett frowned, his arms tightening possessively around her. He kept ignoring that one little fact. She'd wanted to seduce Carl. In the truck, that had made sense. Why not seduce the star athlete, the wealthy lawyer? But to Rachel, Carl was no star. More like the enemy. So what had she been trying to prove?

He moved his hands to her shoulders, pushing her gently away. Her eyes drifted open, dreamy at first, then surprised. "Why did you want to seduce Carl?"

Something akin to fear flashed in her eyes, then vanished. The corner of her mouth curled up into a weak smile. "I don't know what you mean."

With the side of his thumb, he traced her cheekbone. "Sure you do, babe. My ego'd like to believe you were overcome by my rugged good looks and charming personality, but the truth is, you turned on the heat once you thought I was Carl."

The smile faltered. "What difference does it make what I thought your name was?"

"I know what a jerk he was. What were you trying to prove?" That she was good enough for Carl now, even if she hadn't been as a kid?

And did you sleep with me only because you thought I was Carl?

With a twist, she freed herself from his embrace. "I'm...I'm gonna go get a beer."

He caught her hand, urging her back even as he pushed his unwelcome thoughts away. Last night, in the moment, her passion had been as real as his. That was the one undisputable fact, and he kept it front and center in his mind.

He pulled her close and held her tight. Maybe she'd gone into the lion's den thinking Carl was the lion, but in the end, all that had mattered was the way they'd connected, no matter what his identity.

"Garrett," she said, her voice tense and low, "this isn't a slow song."

She was right. The band had replaced the jukebox and was jamming to a countrified rock song. He pulled her closer, still swaying to a nonexistent ballad. "So?"

"People are staring."

He tilted her chin up and smiled. "Sweetheart, people would stare at you no matter what song was playing."

Her cheeks flushed, but she nodded. "The last time I was here nobody would have given me a second look if I'd climbed on stage naked and performed a rain dance."

Probably an exaggeration, though considering what Carl said, maybe not. "Is that why you didn't tell me your name? You wanted to surprise everyone with how much you've changed?"

She frowned. "Sort of. Not entirely."

"Then why?"

"Oh, no." Leaning back against the circle of his arms, she looked up at him. "We had a deal. We dance, you tell me why you let me believe you were Carl."

"I did say that, didn't I?"

"Yes, you did."

A couple whirled by, the woman a flash of red jeans and boots as she almost barreled into Garrett. "Think we can move like that?"

"No," she said with a laugh, "and you're changing the subject." She pressed against him, locking her arms around his waist, her cheek warm against his chest. "We're dancing," she murmured. "So that means you should be talking, remember?"

"I'd rather just hold you." He'd rather do a lot of things, all of which required leaving the dance floor.

"A deal's a deal."

Well, damn. He floundered for words, wanting to make her understand without putting his own heart on the line. "You moved me."

She angled her head back to look at him, one eyebrow raised. "Composing a Barry Manilow song?" she asked, eyes twinkling.

So much for cop-out answers. He framed her face with his hands and looked deep in her eyes. "I wanted you,"

Play The Lucky Hearts Game

and get... FREE BOOKS & a FREE GIFT... YOURS to KEEP!

Yes! I have scratched off the silver card. Please send me my **2 FREE BOOKS** and **FREE MYSTERY GIFT**. I understand that I am under no obligation to purchase any books as explained on the back of this card.

Scratch Here! then look below to see what your cards get you...

342 HDL C6J4   **142 HDL C6JU**

NAME   (PLEASE PRINT CLEARLY)

ADDRESS

APT.#   CITY

STATE/PROV.   ZIP/POSTAL CODE

Twenty-one gets you **2 FREE BOOKS** and a **FREE MYSTERY GIFT!**

Twenty gets you **2 FREE BOOKS!**

Nineteen gets you **1 FREE BOOK!**

TRY AGAIN!

Offer limited to one per household and not valid to current Harlequin Temptation® subscribers. All orders subject to approval.

Visit us online at www.eHarlequin.com

(H-T-OS-10/00)

DETACH AND MAIL CARD TODAY!

The Harlequin Reader Service® — Here's how it works:

Accepting your 2 free books and gift places you under no obligation to buy anything. You may keep the books and gift and return the shipping statement marked "cancel.". If you do not cancel, about a month later we'll send you 4 additional novels and bill you just $3.34 each in the U.S., or $3.80 each in Canada, plus 25¢ shipping & handling per book and applicable taxes if any.* That's the complete price and — compared to cover prices of $3.99 each in the U.S. and $4.50 each in Canada — it's quite a bargain! You may cancel at any time, but if you choose to continue, every month we'll send you 4 more books, which you may either purchase at the discount price or return to us and cancel your subscription.

*Terms and prices subject to change without notice. Sales tax applicable in N.Y. Canadian residents will be charged applicable provincial taxes and GST.

If offer card is missing write to: Harlequin Reader Service, 3010 Walden Ave., P.O. Box 1867, Buffalo NY 14240-1867

BUSINESS REPLY MAIL
FIRST-CLASS MAIL   PERMIT NO. 717   BUFFALO, NY

POSTAGE WILL BE PAID BY ADDRESSEE

HARLEQUIN READER SERVICE
3010 WALDEN AVE
PO BOX 1867
BUFFALO NY 14240-9952

NO POSTAGE
NECESSARY
IF MAILED
IN THE
UNITED STATES

he said simply. She held his gaze, her breath quickening, silently telling him that she'd wanted him, too. "You were a bright spot in an otherwise hideous day. Carl's lying to get me back to Texas, this thing with my father." He held up a hand to ward off her question. "Don't ask. The point is, there you were—a confident, beautiful woman with a sharp tongue and a fast wit. How could I risk letting you get away?"

She broke eye contact to stare toward the floor. "And you thought I'd leave if you weren't Carl?"

"Seemed like the reasonable assumption at first."

"At first?"

"Later, I wasn't thinking much."

"Oh..."

The bandleader announced the Cotton-Eye Joe, and a couple sitting at a nearby table stood and moved to the floor. Since it wouldn't be easy to waltz while the crowd was doing a line dance, Garrett eased Rachel over to the abandoned table. He pulled his chair next to hers and rested one hand on her thigh.

"In a way we both came back for Carl," he said. She frowned, and he reached out to stroke her cheek. "I guess I can't be mad at him anymore since I ended up with you." With his finger, he twirled a strand of her hair. "How about you? Can you still be mad?"

She ran her teeth over her lower lip, then shifted in her chair, finally looking up at him with defiance shining in her eyes. "It's not my turn, cowboy. Remember? I want to hear about the *you weren't thinking* part."

"We're not dancing anymore."

Leaning forward, she swung one hand around his neck, her fingers twining through his hair. "Tell me anyway," she whispered, her breath grazing his ear.

He called on every ounce of his strength to keep from

hauling her onto his lap and kissing her senseless. Hell, if they weren't surrounded by half the town, he would have happily stripped her naked and made love to her on the table.

"I wanted you," he repeated. "Everything about you. Your scent, your taste, your touch. You looked at me and I lost my mind. And, frankly, I didn't give a damn who you thought you were seducing. By the time we were in the clinic, you wanted me, too—really wanted me."

He trailed his finger up her thigh, dangerously close to heaven, his torment hidden from questioning eyes by the plastic tablecloth. She squirmed, her lips parted, her eyes warm. "Tell me I'm right," he demanded, his voice gravelly with need. "You wanted the man—*me*. You weren't interested in the name."

Her eyes were closed, her breathing quick.

"Tell me."

"I wanted you."

"And you still do." He traced a lazy circle on her inner thigh. "You want to finish what we started."

She opened her eyes, and he knew the answer. "I...I'm not sure it's a good idea."

Maybe not, but he was sure she still wanted it. He kissed the corner of her mouth. "I can't think of a better idea."

"I'm not the woman you think I am." She focused on the table, her teeth grazing her lower lip.

"You're traveling incognito?"

That drew a timid smile. "Something like that."

She was wrong, of course. He knew exactly who she was. Maybe she didn't realize it, maybe she wouldn't believe it was true, but they'd torn through barriers and he'd seen a piece of her soul last night. He didn't intend to lose her. Not without a fight.

"I know exactly who you are. I'm more concerned with whether you know me." He swallowed, working up the courage to confess his fear. "I didn't want to believe you'd slept with me only because you thought I was Carl."

"*No.*" The word exploded from her with such force he cringed, wondering what nerve he'd struck. "I never planned to sleep with Carl. *Never.* Not that cree—" She broke off, pressing her lips together in a thin line, then shook her head. "Well, if you thought that's what I wanted, then you *don't* know me. Not at all." She ran a hand through her hair and took a deep breath. "I'm..." She glanced around. "I need to go to the ladies' room."

As she stood up, he reached for her, but she shrugged him off, then weaved her way through the crowd gathered at the edge of the dance floor. He watched her leave, wondering where he'd stumbled. Earlier, she'd more or less admitted to turning on the charm because she thought he was Carl. Maybe she'd been a little embarrassed, but she hadn't stormed off in a huff. No, she hadn't done *that* until he'd suggested she'd intended to sleep with Carl. To Garrett, it seemed the logical termination of a seduction. Apparently Rachel didn't agree. Automatically, he reached for his back pocket for a cigarette, then stopped himself, remembering that he'd quit.

He frowned, staring toward the far side of the bar where she'd disappeared. She was up to something, all right. The answer was right there, so close he could almost grasp it. But that was okay. He wasn't going anywhere.

Sooner or later, he'd figure out her game.

THE REFLECTION in the mirror looked calm and confident, every hair still in place, makeup still flawless.

Proof positive that appearances can be deceiving. She was a million miles from calm and confident. More like frantic and freaked.

Nothing was going right. Instead of simply asking Garrett if Carl would be coming by, she'd let him talk her into dancing. Dancing of all things. Why couldn't he have suggested pool? Or darts? Poker, even. Anything where she could have kept her distance, and kept her head on straight.

As it was, she'd lost herself in his arms, forgetting her mission, forgetting everything except the way he felt and how much she craved him. And like a total dunderhead, she'd gone and admitted to wanting him. "Stupid, stupid, stupid!"

"You okay?"

Her hand flew to her throat and she spun around. The woman from the dance floor stood just inside the doorway, tight red jeans glowing in the dim light.

"You scared me. I didn't hear anyone come in."

The girl smiled. "Sorry. I'm Lucy." She stuck a hand out in greeting, and Rachel shook it, introducing herself as well. "You must be having a fight with your boyfriend."

"I must?"

"I just assumed. I mean, you're all lovey-dovey on the dance floor, and then you're in here beating yourself up."

Lovey-dovey? Mortification engulfed her. "I didn't realize we were making that much of a spectacle."

"Don't worry. I doubt anyone else noticed. I'm a people-watcher. That's polite for nosy." Lucy rummaged in her purse and came out with a compact, then attacked her nose. "So what was the fight about?"

Rachel opened her mouth to tell the woman that it was none of her business. Then she mentally shrugged. Lucy seemed harmless enough. "It wasn't really a fight, and he's not my boyfriend."

Snapping the compact shut, Lucy turned around, eyebrows riding high. "Honey, here in Braemer, when a man wears his woman tighter than his Levi's, we call that a boyfriend."

"He's not. Really. We barely know each other." That was true, even though she felt like she'd known him forever and could talk to him about anything.

In the main room, the music stopped. The door banged open, and a gaggle of women traipsed in, squeezing to share the counter space and mirror.

Lucy dropped the compact in her purse and emerged with a tube of lipstick. "Well, he may not be your boyfriend yet, but he's aiming in that direction." With a practiced hand, she painted her lips the same color as her nails, even while looking sideways at Rachel's reflection. "And you want it too. I can tell these things."

Maybe. But wanting and having were two different things. Even if she wanted Garrett, there was no way that he could want her except in bed. He didn't even know her. He'd confessed as much when he'd admitted to falling for the confident, beautiful woman he'd met on the road.

But that woman wasn't her. Not really. Like all the men she'd pushed away over the years, Garrett wanted Seductress Rachel. He didn't know the woman under the mask existed, and Rachel doubted he'd even want to.

Damn.

Lucy was staring at her, wanting some sort of answer.

"He doesn't really know me," Rachel said. "I think he's got the wrong impression."

A redheaded teenager who must have used a crowbar to get into her Calvin Klein skirt glanced up from her mini-makeover. "The gorgeous guy in the olive green button-down? Man, if he doesn't know you, I'd sure say he wants to."

Her companion grabbed an eyeliner off the counter. "No kidding. If you don't want him, I've got dibs."

Normally, Rachel would be shocked that a sixteen-year-old was ogling a man who had to be about double her age. As it was, she was too mortified that they'd noticed her at all to care that they were lusting after Garrett. She shot a glance toward Lucy. "I thought you said nobody else noticed?"

"Kids notice everything."

Great. Just great.

Skirt Girl looked up. "Kids? I bet our advice would be better than yours." She turned to Rachel. "So what's the problem?"

For crying out loud, this was getting out of control. "Nothing. Really. No problem at all."

She needed to get out of here. They were being perfectly nice, true. But the situation was becoming absurd. Paris giving her advice was one thing. It was completely different to be handed dating tips by a cluster of Braemer girls who had absolutely no idea who she was or what she was doing there.

Dating tips? No, no, no. There was no *dating*. There was Rachel, there was her plan, and there were her victims. That was it. No dating, no relationship.

No Garrett.

The thought depressed her. Maybe she should sneak out a window and find some ice cream.

She took a quick look around and found a tiny window about the size of a cat door. So much for that plan. With a sigh, she took the second best option. She backed into a stall and shut the door, then sat on the toilet lid and waited for the salon session to be over and the ladies' room to clear.

"Seriously, lady—"

"Her name's Rachel," Lucy said helpfully.

"Okay, Rachel," Skirt Girl continued, "I give great advice. I'm practically the Ann Landers of Braemer High."

Rachel buried her face in her hands, wondering if aliens ever kidnapped women from the ladies' room at the Cotton Gin.

"She thinks her boyfriend isn't really interested in her," Lucy said.

"He's not my boyfriend," Rachel called from behind the stall door.

"Oh, well, that's easy," Skirt Girl went on, apparently not impressed with Rachel's denials. "Just get all ga-ga over some other guy. If that doesn't get your boyfriend's juices going, nothing will."

"You go, girl," said the other teenager. "Show him who's boss."

Rachel groaned, and Lucy leaned against the stall, her bright red boots visible under the door. "You gotta admit, Rach, the kid's got a point."

SHE STUCK HER HEAD out of the ladies' room and looked around. No sign of Lucy or Skirt Girl. Good.

She was just about to allow herself a sigh of relief when she saw *him* sitting near the bar nursing a bottle of beer.

Jason Stilwell.

Her stomach roiled and she felt cold. Oh, God.

Immediately, she scanned the room for Garrett, disgusted with herself for wanting his strength, but not disgusted enough to stop looking. She frowned. He wasn't at their table. She glanced over the rest of the room. No Garrett.

So much for Lucy's stellar deductions. Apparently he didn't want her enough to hang around after she'd stormed off.

Not that it mattered. She'd never confront her demons if she clung to Garrett like a shield, no matter how appealing the idea might be. She had her plan, and now one of her victims had walked into her trap.

Okay, then. Time to turn on the charm.

With her fingers, she fluffed up her hair, then licked her lips. She glanced down to make sure her shirt was tucked in, an unnecessary exercise. She'd looked in the mirror five minutes ago and had no complaints. It wasn't as if she'd walked through a windstorm. She was just stalling, and she knew it.

Time to go.

Right. Sure. Except her feet weren't too keen on moving toward the bar. She tried a mental pep talk. Payback, remember? This guy had totally messed with her mind, and now it was time to take her life back.

This time her feet cooperated, and she pushed her way through the crowd toward his table. He looked up as she approached, and she fought revulsion as his eyes took her in. All of her. Slowly, from her toes to her eyes, with a significant pause at chest level. The creep. She had a sudden urge to pull a trenchcoat tight around her, but damn if she wasn't fresh out of coats.

Taking a deep breath, she squared her shoulders and gathered her strength. He was nothing but a pathetic jerk, a man who'd gotten by on his looks and family money. She could handle him. No problem.

She plastered on her best bimbette smile. "You alone?"

"Well, now, I guess I'm not anymore." He patted the seat next to him. "Why don't you just park that little tush of yours right here?"

So far, so good. Except for the fact that he completely repelled her, of course. But that part had been expected.

She parked her tush and upped the wattage on her smile.

A waitress drifted by and Rachel ordered a beer.

Jason downed half a bottle and swallowed a belch. "Make that two."

"Six-fifty."

One beat, then another. No move on Jason's part to pull out a wallet. Apparently, Jason considered himself enough of a catch that the women should pay for the privilege of watching him burp. She shrugged and paid the tab. Whatever. She was here to seduce him, not play Emily Post.

"I haven't seen you here before," he said, though how he would know, Rachel wasn't sure, since he seemed to be checking out her bra size more than her face.

She tried to avoid deep breaths. Wouldn't want to give the guy a coronary. "I just came in today."

That must have been the right answer, because he looked up. "Staying a while, I hope?"

"A few days."

The waitress dropped off their beers, and he took her hand as she reached for her drink. She forced herself to broaden her smile rather than rip her hand away. This was a seduction, after all. He'd hardly buy into the routine if he could tell how much he creeped her out.

He looked at her expectantly, and she realized he'd said something. She leaned forward and laughed, hoping he'd been making an attempt at humor. He didn't look at her like she was nuts, so maybe she'd guessed right.

She tugged her hand free and grabbed her beer, then held it up in a silent toast. They clinked glass and she took a gulp, wishing it were tequila and would anesthetize her.

She couldn't stand this man. She hadn't liked him in school, and she didn't like him now. He was rude and self-centered and not in the least bit interesting. Yet somehow she'd managed to let him steal ten years of her life.

Pathetic.

She pushed the thought away. She'd come here on a mission and she intended to see it through. Once Seductress Rachel saved the day, all the pieces would fall back into place. Belinda Dean would disappear, New York Rachel could tone it down, and she could just be herself. Whoever the hell that was.

But if she didn't go through with her plan, she'd never figure that out. And she desperately needed to—now more than ever. Some tiny part of her wanted to believe Garrett did want her—the real her. But how could she know for sure until she'd clawed through all the layers and shown herself to him?

She eyed Jason, psyching herself up to slather on the charm. She *needed* to see this through. She was just nervous, that's all.

The band finished its set to an enthusiastic round of applause. Someone turned the jukebox back on, and "Crazy" blared out once again. Rachel swallowed.

"Something wrong?"

"It's just that I really like this song." *And the man I danced to it with.*

"So let's dance."

She bit her lip, repulsed by the thought of his arms around her—especially when she was still basking in the glow of Garrett's touch. But this was her mission, and she had to do something.

"I've got a better idea," she said, keeping her voice low and sultry. "Why don't you buy me dinner?" She should add—*and then we'll have our own private dance later*—but she couldn't bring herself to say the words. New York Rachel was losing her edge.

He twisted to survey the room. When his gaze returned to her, she batted her lashes, trying to jump-start her flirting attempts. His expression letting her know he'd got the message.

"Sure thing, sugar. Someplace a little less crowded."

He stood up and wrapped a possessive arm around her waist, practically dragging her toward the door. Mr. Chivalry, he wasn't. In the parking lot, he aimed her toward a classic boat of a car. Rachel grimaced. Probably not a good idea to be cooped up on a bench seat with a horny former football star.

Time for a brilliant change in itinerary, except she was fresh out of ideas.

Someone brushed against her, and then a hand rested on her shoulder. She stiffened, knowing who it had to be.

"You want to take your paws off my date?" Garrett said.

Relief warred with anger, both melting away when she turned around to face him.

He looked wonderful.

He was messing up her plan.

She wanted to hit him. Unfortunately, she also wanted to hold him, kiss him, make love to him. Which meant that her body was receiving some rather conflicting signals.

"Your date?" Angry red crept up Jason's face like a rash. "I didn't see her leaving with you."

Garrett's face tightened. "I guess you weren't looking hard enough." With that, he eased her away from Jason and pulled her close. She gasped, every coherent thought evaporating except for one—Garrett.

"Come on, sweetheart. You're leaving with me."

8

"IN," HE SAID, holding his temper and the passenger door.

She scowled, but didn't argue, and he stalked around the truck to his side.

"What did you think you were doing?" he demanded the second he slid into the cab.

"Me?" she said, her voice squeaking. "I was just talking."

"The hell you were." He shot her a glance. "I know *exactly* what you were doing." He'd figured it out the moment he saw her flirting with Jason, but looking miserable since she obviously thought the man was lower than pond scum.

About that, at least, they were in total agreement.

Now, though, he was faced with the disconcerting realization that seeing her turn on the charm for another man had ripped a hole in his gut. And the fact that she thought the man was slime hadn't made it any better.

She licked her lips and fiddled with the glove box latch. "I don't know what you're talking about."

Garrett knew better, but he wasn't going to argue. Not yet. Not until he could figure out what to do. He grabbed a pack of cigarettes off the seat and tapped one out.

"You smoke?"

He shrugged, tucking the cigarette between his lips. "Not exactly.

"It's a disgusting habit. You should quit."

Great. First Carl, now Rachel. Giving in, he slid the cigarette back into the pack. "I did. I just carry them around."

Her eyes widened. "So you agree it's a gross habit and you don't smoke? And yet you carry around all the accoutrements." She wrinkled her nose. "Cowboy, you need some serious therapy time."

"Me?" He smashed the pack into a ball, then pitched it behind the seat. "See? I can quit. Think you can quit that easily?"

Her eyes widened, and she bit her lip, then tilted her head down and studied her fingernails. So much for diplomacy. Irritated, he fired the ignition and slammed the truck into reverse. He didn't bother to turn the thing around, just backed it all the way out of the lot, cutting dangerously close to Jason, still standing next to his restored Pontiac.

"These things go forward, too, you know."

"Thanks for the tip, sweetheart." He glanced sideways and caught her wary grin. Like she wasn't sure what to make of him. Hell, he wasn't sure either. He was falling for her even while she was driving him crazy, and the sensation was terrifying. Sort of like skydiving without a chute.

They hit the road, and he jammed in the clutch, then shifted into first, working his frustration out on the transmission until they were finally cruising in fourth gear.

Even though he'd figured out her plan, he still couldn't quite believe what she was up to. It was one thing to be angry at the boys who'd tormented her. It was completely different to prance around like Mata Hari on a mission, flirting with them to prove God only knows what.

True, he didn't know her that well. But he knew enough to be certain she'd never come on to Jason Stilwell without an ulterior motive.

Even more, Garrett was sure that her sex kitten gig was just an act. She was playing a role—playing it well, true, but it was still just a façade. His body hardened with the memory of her innocent eyes like warm caramel, the way she'd blushed in his arms. Hardly standard operating procedure for your average woman of the world.

She shifted, and he glanced over. When she tucked a leg under her and sat up, he got the impression she was rallying.

"Okay," she said. "You've got me in here. Do you wanna tell me why?"

Why? Because Jason Stilwell's a prick, that's why, and he couldn't stand to see her that close to such slime. The words screamed through his brain, but instead of saying them, he just said, "We need to talk," and kept on driving toward the Daltons' place. As a kid, he'd spent countless afternoons there talking Carl out of childish pranks. Maybe the place still held some persuasive power.

She sat back, arms crossed over her chest, perfect white teeth tugging at her lower lip. She didn't exactly radiate contentment, but at least she wasn't running screaming from him. Of course, he was doing more than forty. The real test would come when he stopped the truck.

He found the familiar caliche road easily, and turned onto it, the truck bucking beneath them as it maneuvered the ruts and potholes. Lit only by the glow of the full moon, the place looked majestic, not run-down. Still, it was clearly empty, and a surge of relief washed over him. The ramshackle old house was like a dear friend, and he wanted to see it fixed up, but the idea of it belonging to someone else didn't sit well.

"Why are we here?" She was leaning forward, her hands on the dashboard, squinting through the darkness at the house.

"Don't worry. No one's going to come out with a shotgun. It's been abandoned for years."

Twisting in her seat, she aimed a huge smile at him. "I know." She tugged on the broken door handle, but nothing happened. Then she scooted his direction, pushing him with her hip, a live wire filling the cab with energy. "Come on. Get out."

Confused but obedient, he slipped out, then helped her down. "This is my house," she said. "I can't believe you brought me here."

"Yours?"

She flashed him a *duh* look. "Not *mine* mine. I don't own it or anything. But Dex and I used to play here."

Her house? The realization that this place meant as much to her as it did to him warmed him. She was connected to him in so many ways. Carl. This house. Thumper. *His heart.* She'd wormed her way into his life, and he didn't know if she even wanted to be there.

Well, he intended to convince her.

With a quick glance at him, she took off running toward the porch. From the steps, she flashed a genuine smile and he wanted to swell up like a rooster. Damn, but he liked seeing her happy.

"I'll grab a flashlight," he called, then rummaged behind the seat until he found one. He considered pulling the shotgun off the rack, just in case anything too wild decided to join them, but opted against it.

The door pushed open easily, and they stepped inside. It was a small house, but it had once been proud. Even now, the walls stood straight, the banister curved gracefully. "It's like it's waiting for someone who really wants it," she said, and he had to agree.

When she turned to him, eyes shining in the reflected light, he pulled her into the circle of his arms. She tilted her head back and smiled, and his heart swelled.

"Thank you for bringing me here," she said.

"You're welcome."

A cloud crossed her face, and she frowned, that cute little V appearing above her nose. "Why *did* you bring me here?"

He took her hand and urged her to the staircase, settling beside her on the first step. "Like I said, we need to talk."

"About what?" She made the inquiry lightly, but he could hear the wariness lacing her voice.

"I think you know." He wondered if his voice conveyed just how much he wanted her, how much she'd come to mean to him in such a very short time.

Her eyes widened and she stood up, then began pacing in front of him. "I'm sure I don't."

He frowned. He was never going to get close if she kept running away. He knew she was fragile, scared of how she felt about him and determined to get even with Jason and Derek. *And Carl.*

What he needed was a plan, something that would keep them together without investing her heart. Something that would entice her, but wouldn't terrify her. Something pure and simple.

Something like sex.

Okay, he could do that. He bit back a wry grin. Anything for the cause.

"Then let me lay it out for you," he said. "I want you. In my bed. Right now." That was only half the truth, but something told him she could handle the sex. That she *wanted* it. The rest of it would be harder. The part where he wanted her to open her heart to him and forget about her scheme.

She kept her back straight, the picture of rigid aloofness. But her eyes told a different story, and he pressed his advantage.

"I want to finish what we started. And so do you."

For just a moment, he wondered if he was being smart. After all, his life really didn't need any more complications, and this woman was certainly turning out to be complicated. And yet he couldn't have walked away if he wanted to. Just the opposite, in fact. His heart had switched to autopilot, zeroing in on Rachel Dean. He wasn't prepared to examine the future. But right then, he wanted her. And he intended to do whatever was necessary to get her.

She stood up, taking a baby step away from him. Instantly, he was on his feet, closing the distance.

"You know you want to." He traced her cheekbone, then trailed his finger off her face to land lightly on her shoulder. Hoping he was making her as crazy as himself, he continued the trek, his fingertip following the outline of her bra strap to the swell of her breast.

"Garrett, please." She nibbled her lower lip, then glanced down toward his hand, her breath coming fast and uneven. "You're not playing fair."

"I'm not trying to play fair," he whispered. He moved his hand to her elbow and urged her toward him, trying to ignore the surge of electricity that strengthened as the space between their bodies closed. "I'm trying to keep you around."

Slowly, she raised her head and met his gaze. The battle playing out on her face was obvious—satisfy her need and stay with him, or continue with her absurd game and leave. He held his breath, silently willing her to stay.

"We had a wonderful night. Truly." She licked her lips and he heard a *but* coming on. "It's just that you don't really know me at all."

Wrong answer. "That's part of the fun, sweetheart." He kissed the tip of his index finger, then traced her perfect lips. "I'm looking forward to making the acquaintance of every single part of you."

"What if I were to say that I don't want you to?"

He grinned, not believing her for a minute. "Is that something you're likely to say?"

It was a dangerous question, and he held his breath. Then she closed her eyes and, ever so slightly, shook her head. "No."

Garrett exhaled, dizzy with relief. "Don't I owe you a dance?"

She glanced around, indecision playing across her face. Then she moved into his arms, a definite step in the right direction. He mentally added a tick mark to his internal scoreboard. Chalk one up for the home team.

"You were wrong to pull me away from Jason." Her words caressed his neck, taking the sting out of her meaning.

"Sweetheart, you should just walk away. It's been ten years. Forgiveness is the milk of all kindness, and junk like that."

"That makes no sense at all." She tilted her head back and faced him, her eyes hard and determined. "Besides,

I have a plan. A mission. I'm going to be just fine, and it's really not your concern."

She might have a mission, but so did he. And Garrett didn't intend to lose.

"A woman with a purpose," he said with a grin.

"Something like that." She leaned back and smiled as his heart did a little number in his chest.

"Suppose I could help," he said, leading her to the stairs and up to the first landing. "Would you let me?"

"I don't know how you would."

"Then I'll show you." He ran his hand from the base of her neck up through her hair, twisting the silken strands around his fingers. Then he sat down, pulling her into the V between his legs. "Remember the way you let me help you on the road?" With one hand, he stroked her breast through her shirt, his movements both a tease and a promise.

"Garrett," she said, her voice low, desperate. "I don't—"

"Shhh," he whispered, his lips grazing the back of her ear. "And in the clinic, don't you remember how I helped you forget your troubles?" He trailed his hand down, toying with the button on her jeans until it released and he could coax the zipper down. Her breath quickened, and she squirmed, her subtle movements helping as he slipped his hand lower, under the silk of her panties, and finally fingered her soft curls.

With his arm around her waist, he urged her closer, wanting to feel her delicious rear pressed tight between his legs. Already, his body throbbed. God, he wanted this woman.

With his other hand, he continued to administer his own form of sweet torture, and he dipped his fingertip lower, teasing and enticing, but still only hinting.

"Garrett," she moaned, pressing back against him. Her hands were on his thighs, and her fingers pressed into his leg. "Please..."

He called upon every ounce of his strength to pull his hand away and not make love to her on the dusty floor. She whimpered, protesting, and he knew he wasn't making it easier on her—or on himself—but her plan was ridiculous, and he had to figure out just the right way to pitch his idea.

She wanted Jason and Derek, and he'd help her get them. More or less, anyway. If he played his cards right, there wouldn't be a moment when Rachel wasn't in his bed or on his arm. Hopefully, that would give him enough time to convince her to abandon her ridiculous scheme.

He had only one chance to convince her, and he didn't intend to blow it. With the tip of his tongue, he caressed the curve of her ear. She trembled against him, and he held her close. "Let me help you now, Rachel. Let me tell you how."

She drew in a shuddered breath, the pulse in her neck quickening under his hand. "I...I need...I need some air." Then she moved away, pushing herself up.

He followed her outside, joining her on the front stoop of the old house. Trying for nonchalance, he picked up her hand and held it in his lap, thrilled that she didn't pull away.

He took a breath. Now or never.

"Jason's already frustrated as hell," he said. Her eyes widened, but Garrett didn't pause. "You saw the way he watched you as we drove away. So you're halfway home."

She gaped, the full import of Garrett's words hitting

her with enough force to quell the sweet, lingering memory of his hands stroking and teasing her.

He really did know exactly what she was up to.

He couldn't.

But he did. Somehow he'd figured it out.

She considered denying everything, but quickly ruled that out. Better to tackle the problem head-on.

Calling on all her courage, she looked him straight in the eye. "Okay, cowboy. Tell me." She fought to keep her voice steady. "What did you have in mind?"

The corner of his mouth twitched, and she knew he was fighting a grin.

"I'll be your red herring."

When he grinned, a small dimple appeared in his cheek and she had an overwhelming urge to kiss it. *Down, girl.* If she concentrated, she could keep her lust under control. And that was all it was—just lust. An undeniable chemistry sparked between them, but that was hardly a solid enough reason to back off a plan she'd spent half a continent perfecting. She'd lost her head back in the house, true, but she didn't intend to lose it again.

Still...*oh, Lord*...if he could scratch that itch...

She pressed her thighs tight together, the memory of his touch so vivid she could still feel him. She wanted him. Wanted to snuggle up next to him, naked and warm and safe.

"Rach?"

She blinked. Her mind had been wandering. From his tone, she'd bet he knew exactly where her thoughts had drifted. She plastered on a dubious expression and tried to regroup. "What are you talking about?"

He scooted closer, until his face was just inches from

her. He smelled male, all spice and beer and need. It was everything she could do not to kiss him, not to beg him.

"The whole idea is to make the men want you, right?" he asked, his voice like warm syrup.

Once again she considered denial as a reasonable course of conduct, and once again she ruled it out. Nope, better to just take the bull by its proverbial horns. She raised an eyebrow and licked her lips, enjoying the reaction she saw in his eyes. "How about you?" She pitched her voice low. "Do you want me?"

She'd meant it as a tease, but immediately regretted the words. From the fire in his eyes, she knew the answer. "Never mind," she said, backpedalling. Flirting with Garrett was a mistake. She knew where it could lead and—as much as she wanted to finish what they'd started—it just wasn't a good idea. "Just tell me your plan."

He flashed a cat-who-swallowed-the-canary grin. "Stilwell thought you were hot in the bar. But as soon as I took you away, you became a much hotter commodity because I've got you and he doesn't."

"Oh no," she said, suddenly sure that she knew what he was up to. "I don't think so."

"Don't think so what?"

"Whatever you've got up your sleeve," she answered, evading the question just in case she'd imagined something more wild that what he had in mind.

He clasped her one hand between his two. "Then let me tell you exactly what I'm suggesting, so that you know exactly what you're turning down."

Swallowing, she nodded. Nearby an owl hooted, and a deer stepped out from the tree line. Apparently, every animal in the county was as intrigued by his proposition as she was.

"You want him lusting after you, jealous, practically drooling whenever he looks your direction. Right?"

It sounded pretty pitiful when he put it that way, but he'd more or less summed up her plan. She nodded.

"Well, what better way to make him and Derek Booker—"

She gasped. She hadn't realized how much he'd figured out.

"—insane with lust than to be constantly, *affectionately*, on the arm of another man."

Her mouth curled. "Namely you."

"You got it, sweetheart."

"Just how affectionate are we talking?"

"*Very* affectionate," he said, and Rachel's stomach did a nosedive. She pulled her hand free, needing the distance, afraid that if she continued to touch him she'd never stop.

His plan was perverse, but it just might work. In fact, Skirt Girl had suggested almost the same thing. Except she'd expected Rachel to flirt with someone other than Garrett—the idea being that Garrett would get all hot and bothered, realize how much he needed Rachel, and they'd run off to live happily ever after.

As appealing as that scenario might be, Rachel was pragmatic enough to know that happily ever after with Garrett wasn't in the game plan. But that was for the best. After all, she lived a continent away from him, and she knew better than to believe in fairy tales. Paris might have made out like a bandit in the relationship department, but Rachel wasn't that lucky. And right now she had bigger problems. Like tackling her mission, assassinating a few personal demons, then getting back to New York and—finally—getting on with her life.

Garrett was just an added benefit in the meantime. A

perk. Like hot fudge on ice cream. Delicious while it lasted. A short but sweet experience.

Except Rachel wasn't so sure if she'd be satisfied with *short*.

"Well?"

He looked sincere. He even looked like he wanted to be helpful. And she had to admit his plan made sense in a perverse, weird sort of way.

Even though it would only be for show, she still shivered, imagining his arms wrapped around her, his lips caressing her. She'd told herself she wouldn't pursue a relationship with him, that she couldn't trust him. But this wasn't a relationship. It was an act. Just another plot twist in the farce she already had going.

Like he'd said, he'd be her red herring, the pretend boyfriend. Arm candy. Nothing about him would be real. They'd finish what they'd started, but it would just be lust and sex. Sadness tweaked in her stomach, but she told herself that was okay. That made it easier to keep her distance. That made it safe.

He was waiting patiently for her decision.

Something he'd said earlier rang in her memory. "Jason and Derek. What about Carl?"

A muscle in his cheek twitched. "No Carl. Carl's sorry, you can trust me on that. You're going to have to forget him."

"Are you nuts? He's Victim Number One." She didn't mention he was actually Reinstated Victim Number One, having been slashed from the lineup after her little mix-up with Garrett.

"Now he's not."

Oh.

She frowned, not sure what to argue next. Considering Garrett already thought her plan bordered on lunacy, she doubted he'd be bowled over by a logical approach.

She nibbled on her lower lip. She'd come back to prove a point, true. But in reality, her plan would work with just Jason and Derek. Surely she could get the message across just as well with two victims instead of three. Right? Sure. No problem.

And Carl had been okay all of senior year up until the prom. So he was probably entitled to a commuted sentence. Or at least special dispensation since he was Garrett's brother.

She mentally rolled her eyes. *Carl* wasn't the issue. Garrett was. If she wanted Garrett, she had to give up Carl.

"What if I say no?" she asked, just in case.

"You either take me and forget about Carl, or you go after Carl and I walk."

Not much of a contest. Now that she'd mulled over his offer, the idea of letting her hot fudge sundae get away didn't sit well at all. And considering how much she'd botched her first attempt, she wasn't real keen on seeing what kind of mischief she'd stir up if she took a second go at Carl.

"Okay. It's a deal." She stuck her hand out, waiting for a handshake to seal the bargain.

He just glanced at her out-thrust hand, his brow crinkled. "There's just one little caveat I haven't mentioned yet."

Warning bells rang in her ears. She pulled her hand back and cocked her head, waiting. Wary.

"I want you."

She frowned, confused. "So you said. You want to finish what we started."

"Not an ending. A beginning. I want you in my bed. All the time."

Oh, my. Licking her lips, she forced herself to breathe. She was afraid to ask what he meant, afraid she'd misunderstood.

"I don't do method acting. So while we're putting on this little public show, I want you whenever and however I say." He caught her in his gaze, his blue eyes seeing all her secrets. "And that includes right now. In my bed and naked."

He paused and she let his words creep under her skin and tingle like the buzz of fine wine. His demand surprised and scared her. It also enticed her. To be that close to him, to touch him over and over—*and to do it guilt-free because it was part of their deal.* Well, that was almost too good to pass up.

Almost.

There was the flip side to think about, too. If they were that close, that intimate, then surely he'd figure out she wasn't really Seductress Rachel. Would he still want her when he realized she wore an air of confidence like armor, but underneath she was as soft and insecure as she'd been ten years ago?

God, she was pitiful. For fifteen hundred miles she'd told herself the reason for coming back was to prove she'd changed. Really changed. She *was* confident. She *was* hot. She *was* sexy. Belinda Rachel was dead and Rachel Dean had taken over.

She sighed. How could she convince the town if she couldn't even convince herself?

He'd been watching her, and now he smiled, a professional businessman's smile.

Then he was right there, gripping her arms, holding her in place. She gasped and his mouth found hers. His tongue demanded entrance, and she parted her lips to taste heaven.

His hands on her skin were like fire, shooting a liquid heat through her body that collected just above her thighs. Warm and wanting. And when he pulled away, she heard a whimper and realized it came from her.

"My room, my bed. Now." He paused, a slow smile spreading across his face. "So," he finally said, "do we have a deal?"

9

A TINY SMILE DANCED at the corner of her mouth. "Sorry, your deal won't fly. I can't go with you to your room."

His heart stopped. That couldn't be right. He opened his mouth to say so, to beg, *to grovel*, but she cut him off.

"When we get back to Mrs. Kelley's, we need to go to *my* room." When she took his hand, the corners of her eyes crinkled with silent laughter. "And I need you to check on Thumper."

Relief swept over him. He should have known she'd worry about her dog. He stood up, pulling her to her feet, holding her gaze. He traced the curve of her face. "You can tease all you want," he said, "so long as in the end you're next to me."

Her cheeks flushed pink but she didn't look away. Instead, she closed her hand over his finger and guided it toward her mouth. Tilting her head, she ran her lips over the pad of his finger, then kissed his palm. "Constantly and affectionately, remember?" she murmured against his skin.

She took his finger in her mouth again, drawing him in. He closed his eyes and swallowed as her tongue wreaked havoc with his entire body. His bed was looking less and less necessary. The musty old house would do fine.

She pulled away, and he mourned the distance.

"I have a few conditions of my own," she said.

She avoided his eyes, and Garrett hoped she was beginning to question the wisdom of her sex-kitten scheme. "What kind of conditions?"

"It's about my plan," she said, twisting her hands together. "Jason and Derek. I'm not going to get their juices flowing if they don't see me, right?"

He nodded, wondering what she was leading up to.

"It's not enough to just maybe run into these guys." She licked her lips, hesitating. "So...um...I want you to take me around, arrange meetings so I can...you know." She caught his gaze for just an instant, then her eyes darted away.

He didn't say a word. It was her scheme; she could damn well spell it out.

She cleared her throat. "The thing is, I want them to think they stand a chance. So, if you'd...I mean, I'd like you..."

He sighed. So much for spelling it out. "You want us to put on a show like that number you did with my finger just now, and then you want me to make myself scarce so that they can try to hone in on the action."

As her teeth grazed her lip, she lifted a shoulder. "Yeah."

"Fine." What else could he say? If he didn't agree, she'd pull the plug entirely.

Her brow furrowed. Had she assumed he'd put up a fight? Risk her walking away entirely?

Not hardly.

"But you don't approve." It was a statement, not a question, and he didn't argue. "So why are you helping me?"

"I told you. I want you."

She nodded, apparently satisfied. And why shouldn't

she be? It was the truth, after all. He wanted her with an urgency he'd never experienced before.

So what if it wasn't the whole truth? The full truth would only muddy the waters.

The simple fact was that he had every intention of convincing her to drop her ludicrous plan—just as soon as he figured out how.

THEY'D BEEN IN THE TRUCK only five minutes, and his guilt was already setting in.

From the driver's seat, he cast a sideways glance toward Rachel, who looked to be shifting into sexpot mode. She'd pulled down the visor and was using the tiny mirror to primp—freshening her makeup, brushing her hair. She caught him looking and flashed a smile that promised sex and sin.

He sighed. Somewhere between the house and mile marker 278, he'd lost the real Rachel. The Rachel he wanted—sassy and sweet and alluring as hell—kept ratcheting up the temptress factor. Maybe she thought she needed to prove something to Derek and Jason, but why did she have to prove it to him?

Because that's what she thinks you want, you dumbass.

He'd fallen for her seduction routine last night, and then he'd gone and practically blackmailed her into being his sex slave. Of course she'd assume he was looking for a hot time with a wild woman. It wasn't as if he'd tried to court her with wine and roses. And how would she know he thought she was just as sexy in scrubs as in a tight skirt and two-inch make-out pumps?

Even worse, since he'd practically forced her to play sex kitten, she didn't have to acknowledge how much she wanted him, too. Without thinking, he'd handed her the perfect excuse to keep hiding behind walls. Major dumb-ass maneuver.

So much for acting on the spur of the moment. Now he had to backtrack, because he didn't intend to spend the rest of his life with Mata Hari.

As they passed by the turnoff to Main Street, inspiration struck. *Chivalry.* He'd take her out for a late dinner. Wine and roses, or Braemer's equivalent anyway. He'd apologize for twisting her arm to get her in bed. Then he'd let her know in no uncertain terms that his door would be wide open, and the sheets would be warm whenever she was ready.

Eventually she'd come to him.

And if she didn't?

Then he'd be kicking himself for the rest of his life.

The thought was almost enough to make him screw chivalry, take her home, and throw her onto the bed. Almost, but not quite.

"What are you doing?" she asked as he hit the brakes and spun the steering wheel.

"A brief detour." He finished the U-turn and nodded toward the dim lights coming from the square. Taking his eyes off the road, he glanced at her just long enough to gauge her reaction.

Her brows were furrowed, the little crease was back above her nose. "Oh. I thought you wanted to..." She shifted in her seat. "I thought we were going, you know, to the Bluebonnet."

Garrett just shrugged and turned onto Main Street, hoping he seemed nonchalant even though, on the inside, he was giving himself hearty slaps on the back. Not only had her tone left no doubt that she'd anticipated very specific activities once they arrived at Mrs. Kelley's, but, more importantly, she sounded disappointed that they weren't going straight there.

Hell, in a way he was disappointed, too. If his plan backfired, he might miss out on having her in his bed again. The possibility of not feeling her warm flesh against his skin, not hearing her moan into his ear, not having her beg him for a little more—hell. Maybe this new plan wasn't so great after all.

Frustrated, he spun the steering wheel, sending gravel kicking out from under his tires as he slid the truck to a rough stop in an empty space. "Okay. Here we are."

She peered out the window. "The courthouse?"

Shoving open his door, he nodded. "I want to buy you dinner. I thought we'd walk." In truth, this wasn't where he'd intended to go, but he needed to get out of the cab. Her nearness was making him nuts. He nodded toward her door. "Hold on. I'll let you out."

He circled the truck, letting the soft breeze work on clearing his head. Just knowing that he was consciously and deliberately walking away from a night with Rachel—warm and willing and naked under him—convinced him that he was a total idiot. If any of his college buddies had walked away from a willing woman, they would have suffered no end of jeering.

So why was he risking forfeiture of his Red-Blooded American Male membership card?

Because you're in love with her.

He stopped dead and put a hand on the hood to steady himself. *Love?* That couldn't be right. Could it?

Still pondering that news flash, he stalked to her door, grabbed the handle and yanked it open.

"What's that all about?" she asked, balancing on his arm as she stepped out of the truck.

"What?" he asked, knowing exactly what she was talking about.

"The look on your face. Like you just stepped into *The Twilight Zone*."

"Nothing," he said, trying to school his face into some sort of bland, noncommittal expression. True, he wanted her, even craved her. She fascinated and excited him. But in love? No way. In lust, maybe. Well, probably.

Definitely.

Just lust.

Except somehow he didn't quite believe that.

With a shove, he slammed her door, sending the glass rattling in the window.

She cocked an eyebrow, but didn't press. In silence, they crossed the street. Ephron Booker, Derek's dad, was trying to drag a dry goods display through the front door of the darkened store.

"Hey, Mr. Booker. Need a hand?"

Ephron looked up. "Carl?"

"Garrett," he said.

The older man squinted. "So it is. Haven't seen you around for a while. You filling in while your dad's laid up?"

"Something like that."

"Nice of you to help, boy. I didn't know you and your dad had patched things up."

Rachel quirked an eyebrow at him, then turned to face Ephron. "They're working on it," she said dryly. "Garrett's a forgive-and-forget kind of guy."

He grimaced, not really interested in exploring *that* topic, and picked up the far side of the case. He and Ephron maneuvered it into the store and got it settled. Through the window, he could see Rachel standing on the sidewalk, her finger idly tracing a path around the

sandwich board sign announcing *Booker's General Store,*
Specials Daily. After a moment, she glanced up and
caught his eye. A thin, melancholy smile touched her
lips, and he wondered if she was thinking about forgiving and forgetting. Probably not, but she should be. Hell,
maybe he should be, too.

Sighing, he let his gaze roam over the inside of the
store. One long counter stretched across the far wall, balanced at one end with a push-button cash register that
belonged more in the Smithsonian than in Braemer. A
metal candy rack that Garrett recalled from his childhood stood regally at the far end. The place still smelled
of peppermint and tobacco, and the sign posted behind
the counter announced that the live bait was kept behind
the store. The only clue that Ephron and Braemer had
made a concession to the new millennium was the ATM
machine tucked in by the ice cream freezer.

Ephron headed back to the door and Garrett followed,
only then noticing a few bundles of fresh flowers in tubs
by the window. "How much for one of those?"

"I only sell fresh, so you just go on and help yourself.
These leftovers'll go to the nursing home in the mor-
nin'."

"Thanks." He picked out a bundle of violets. Roses
weren't unique enough for Rachel. But violets, well, they
had definite personality.

When he handed them to her, she opened her mouth
but didn't say anything. Then she bent over to smell
them. When she lifted her face, he could see the smile in
her eyes.

"Thank you." Her cheeks colored under the yellow
sulphur street lights.

"Who's your lady friend?"

Garrett turned back to Ephron. "Rachel Dean. She's in town for the reunion."

The older man ripped open a packet of tobacco with his teeth, then spit toward the gutter. "Rachel Dean. Not little Belinda Rachel?"

Her face went tight. "Yes, sir."

Ephron placed a bony finger under Rachel's chin and tilted her head up. She started at his touch but didn't break contact. "I hope you have a right nice reunion, young lady."

She mumbled something that could have been thanks.

"I always did like your mother. Sure was sorry for all her troubles." He eyed her. "I always hoped she managed to make a good life for herself. Where'd she end up?"

"Dallas." One flat, staccato word.

Ephron nodded. "Glad to hear it. She needed out of Braemer. Couldn't stand the place. Got to be of a mind to appreciate it." He winked. "I've been appreciating the ATM and the new computers at the library myself. Did you know I can order all my stock over the Internet? 'Course that's just an excuse. Mostly I go to those chat rooms."

Garrett chuckled.

"Yup, Braemer's getting to be quite modern. Not like Dallas, though." He shifted his gaze to Rachel again. "So I take it your mother's enjoying life in the big city?"

Her polite smile looked more like a grimace. "She died a while back," she said, her voice catching. "An accident."

Except for the catch, her tone stayed matter-of-fact. But Garrett heard the pain underneath, and he wanted to gather her to him and rock her back and forth. He wanted to make it all better for the lonely little girl and the even lonelier woman she'd become. He had no idea if they'd been close, but it didn't really matter. He wasn't exactly tight with his dad, yet losing him would tear him apart.

After Ephron offered his condolences, they turned to leave. Once they were out of earshot, she turned to Garrett, eyes flashing. "Why did you tell him my name?" Her voice trembled.

He feigned innocence. "What else would I call you?"

"I wanted to be anonymous." She scowled at him. "And now Derek's dad knows I'm in town. That's just great."

He took her hand, twining his fingers between hers, just two former Braemer-ites strolling around the town square. "Wouldn't it be better to let it go? To just go to the reunion and let everyone see how you've changed and start over fresh? Maybe folks would surprise you."

She stopped, pulling him to a halt beside her. When he looked into her eyes he saw determination—and something else. Challenge, maybe?

Squaring her shoulders she trapped him with her gaze. "Is that what you're doing with your dad? Are you starting over fresh, figuring maybe he'll surprise you?"

If what Jennie and Carl said was true, his dad had already surprised him. Not that he was inclined to point that out to Rachel. If she wanted to ponder forgiveness, he was all for it. "Should I be?" he asked. "Forgiving and forgetting? Didn't you tell Ephron that's my new motto?"

"You seem to think it should be mine. What's good for the goose and all that." She shrugged. "Anyway, maybe it *should* be your motto. I mean, he's your dad."

"You have no idea what kind of crap I put up with from him."

"At least you have a dad. Mine disappeared."

"And if he came back, you'd forgive him? Just like that?"

Pursing her lips, she nodded slowly. "I think so. Maybe." She caught his eye. "Yeah. I would."

"Forgive and forget, huh?"

She nodded.

He almost let out a victory whoop. He had her now. "Not exactly practicing what you preach."

Again, her lips pressed thin. "That's different. It's not family."

He opened his mouth to argue, to drive his point home. But she turned and walked on down the sidewalk, finally stopping at the corner and turning back to look at him over her shoulder. "Topic closed, okay?"

"Fine," he said. "Does the topic include your mom?"

"Excuse me?"

"I just wanted to say I'm sorry." Actually, he wanted so much more. He wanted her to open up, to share the hurt he'd heard in her voice.

For a moment, she tensed, and he feared she was going to lash out. Then her shoulders sagged as her lips drew together into a thin line.

"When I heard the news, I couldn't believe she was gone. Except for Paris, my mom was the one steady thing in my life."

"You told her about Jason and Derek?" Surely her mom would have done something to stop their harassment.

Rachel shook her head. "Mom had plenty of worries without my battles, too. She worked at the Tasty Creme during the day and the café at night. And when she got home, she'd go over my homework with me."

"Two jobs?"

She shrugged. "My dad ran off with everything, and totally screwed up her credit. And Mom wanted out of this town. She saved every penny." A tiny smile tugged at her mouth.

"What?"

"Dexter," she said, then the smile blossomed. "Even though we couldn't really afford a dog, she let me have him anyway. I think she could tell how much I wanted him."

"She sounds great," he said, meaning it.

She blinked, and he saw the hint of a tear. "Yeah, well, now the topic is really closed. Okay?"

He nodded. She stared at him for a moment, then smiled.

"So, are you buying me dinner or what?"

EXCEPT FOR THE PORCH LIGHT, the Bluebonnet was dark by the time they got back. Garrett unlocked the door, then followed her inside. No one around. Rachel breathed a sigh of relief. She wasn't inclined to explain her late night activities to Mrs. Kelley.

"After you," he said, placing a gentle hand against her back.

She nodded and led the way, trying to act nonchalant, hoping he couldn't tell that the only thing she wanted to do was get through her door and collapse into his arms.

He hadn't brought up forgiving Jason and Derek again, and she was grateful. A nagging voice kept urging that maybe he was right, and she kept trying to ignore the voice. But with Garrett, it had been easy to forget Jason, Derek and the reunion dance looming in the not-so-distant future.

He'd bought her flowers, held her hand, and then shared a chocolate milkshake at Anabel's Café with her.

One big glass, one cherry, whipped cream and two straws. He'd pulled the cherry off, swathed it with cream, then dangled it in front of her mouth until she'd managed to catch it with her tongue. No easy task since he kept pulling it away. In fact, most of the whipped cream had ended up on her nose, not in her mouth.

Once she'd swallowed the cherry, they'd leaned over the frosty glass, holding hands across the table, and sipped through their straws until the food had arrived. She'd only had three sips of the forbidden treat—rules were rules—but it was the thought that counted.

She had no idea what Garrett was up to, but she liked it. She could spend a lot of happy hours thinking about sharing a shake with Garrett. For that matter, she could happily think about a lot of things with Garrett. He made everything seem different, better. Derek's father had actually been sweet. Anabel's Café had seemed warm and welcome, not cold and chiding.

The whole town seemed nicer when he was around. And for the first time in a long time, she'd spent an evening not worrying about playing a part or turning on the charm. *Amazing.*

Maybe Garrett was the human version of rose-colored glasses.

Rachel paused in front of her room, Garrett so close behind her that his breath stirred the loose hairs at the nape of her neck. On a scale of one to ten, Rachel's nervousness ranked somewhere around eighty-seven.

As she pulled the key out of her purse, he caught her arm and she looked up, expecting fire in his eyes.

Instead, she saw an apology.

"You're amazing, Rach."

He reached out and stroked her cheek, and it was everything she could do not to beg him to take her right there against the door to her room.

Blinking, she forced her way back to reality, fighting the dread congealing in her stomach. "What's wrong?" Her voice sounded small, frantic.

"I'm going to come in and check on Thumper, but then I'd better head on up to my room."

She froze. Somehow, he'd seen shades of Belinda, and now he didn't want her anymore. Her blood ran cold—something she'd never believed happened to real people.

"It's getting late," he said. "You probably want to get some sleep."

"Sleep? I...I thought..."

Her eyes welled, and she blinked, refusing to cry in front of him. He wasn't any better than Carl, leading her on only to dump her at the last minute.

She took a shaky breath. No matter how low he'd made her feel, she wasn't about to shed one more tear for a MacLean. Better to be nonchalant. Let him think it didn't matter.

And it didn't. *Really.*

Garrett MacLean had been fun while he'd lasted. But she didn't need him. Not really.

She bit the inside of her cheek, wondering why she didn't believe that.

Calling on every bit of her willpower, she flipped her hair back and pasted on a confident smile. No sense letting him know she hurt.

"I thought we'd come to an agreement. I guess *however* and *whenever* you want isn't here and now." Taking a deep breath, she slid into the seductress role she'd rehearsed so well, the role she was sure he wanted. She trailed a finger down the front of his shirt, stopping at his belt buckle and hooking the tip of her finger under his waistband.

"Is that what you think?" he asked, his voice on edge.

"What else would I think? You're the one walking away." Trying to make him crazy, she dragged her finger along the top of his waistband. "But just remember that we made a deal. Tomorrow, we meet up with Jason and Derek." The dance was drawing closer, after all. She needed to make some serious progress on her plan.

In the dim light, his blue eyes flashed dark and dangerous. With one fluid motion, he trapped her hand under his own, pressing her palm down against his belt buckle. She gasped, but he wasn't through. With his eyes locked on hers, he slid their joined hands down, lower and lower, until her mind screamed that she couldn't touch him so intimately and not have him.

Under his sensual direction, her palm grazed over the rough denim until he was right there, thick and hot under her hand. She groaned, wanting his jeans to evaporate, wishing the walls would disappear, so she could be naked in bed with him and he could be inside her, loving her and making her crazy.

Reading her mind, he used his free hand to grab her rear and force her entire body closer, trapping their joined hands. Between them, he began to close his own hand so that her fingers were forced to curve around his hard length straining against the rough denim.

She moaned, a small breathy noise, as her own body ignited. His body against her felt wonderful, like heaven, and she shifted until his hand on hers was no longer trapped against her thigh. Now, the back of his hand touched her intimately. Shameless, she moved against him, wanting this man more than she'd ever wanted any other.

"Sweetheart," he said, his voice rough against her ear, "whenever I want is right now."

A burst of pure feminine satisfaction flowed through her. He twisted his hand to cup her sex, stroking her through her jeans, warming her insides. "However is a little different."

The satisfaction turned to confusion. "What do you mean?"

He stepped back then, and she managed to keep from crying out in frustration. "I want you more than I think I've ever wanted any woman."

"Then why—"

"I want you to want me."

I do, she said, then realized no words had come out.

His smile told her he'd understood. "Show me." One finger teased her lower lip. "I'll help you with Jason and Derek, if that's what you really want. But I should never have insisted you sleep with me, no matter how much I want you in my bed."

As she gaped at him, he took her key and opened the door, then guided her into the room as Thumper whined a sleepy greeting. The dog trotted over, toenails clicking. Rachel smiled, feeling oddly maternal as she knelt down and ruffled the fur behind his ears, setting off a flurry of tail wagging. After a few hefty scratches, he let out a little doggy sigh.

"Looks like he's happy to see you," Garrett said, kneeling down to examine the bandaged leg.

At least someone is, she almost snapped. She couldn't remember feeling this sexually overwrought since...well, never. And Garrett's proximity, even while he was doing clinical vet things, wasn't helping her body temperature return to normal.

So she just stood there, wishing he'd either strip her

clothes off and take her right there on the bed, or hurry up and get out of there so she could take an ice-cold shower—but not really wanting the last one at all.

"He looks good. I'm working in the clinic until noon tomorrow. I'll bring back some fresh bandages and some antibiotics, but he's fine for the night." His gaze swept the room. "Have you got any dog food?"

"Just yours. I probably still owe you." Sheepish, she nodded toward the bureau, and he opened the top drawer, revealing the bag of kibble she'd filched from his dad's clinic.

"Most people unpack clothes."

She smirked. "I'm not most people."

In one long stride he was beside her. He ran his hand along the back of her neck, and she shivered under his touch. "No, you're not," he said before turning to leave.

He paused in the doorway. "The ball's in your court, Rach. I don't want to pressure you. If you want me, you let me know and I'll come running. Fast."

He held a hand out to her, and she almost tripped over herself trying to get to his side.

"And if you're too shy to tell me out loud," he said, taking her hand, "then you can always follow Tony Orlando's advice."

Then he kissed her earlobe, sending so many sparks shooting down her body she forgot to ask what Tony Orlando had to do with anything. By the time she got her senses back, he was out the door and down the hall.

10

HE DIDN'T WANT to pressure her? What kind of backwards bullshit was that?

Rachel stared at Garrett's retreating back, sure that her mouth was hanging open. She *wanted* pressure, even welcomed it.

Talk about your unexpected turn of events.

Sighing, she shut the door, then pressed her back against it. Thumper glanced up from his rug, his head cocked, ears twitching.

"He's going to drive me nuts," she told the dog.

Thrilled to be part of the conversation, Thumper started his tail beating a rhythm on the wooden floor.

She slid down the door, her knees up near her chest, and patted the floor beside her. Thumper blinked, then wandered over to curl up at her feet.

"It's you and me, kid," she said, scratching behind his ears. Just like it had been her and Dexter after Paris had moved away.

She eyed the phone. Thumper whined. "It's not you. I just wonder if I don't need an expert opinion here."

Pretty pitiful, really, that at every major crisis in her life she either turned to her dog or made a long-distance phone call. Of course, that would mean that this was a crisis, and it really wasn't. Was it?

She snorted. Hell, yes it was. Reality was sliding out from under her. She no longer knew what to do. For ten years she'd had social etiquette down pat. In New York, she knew how to behave, what to say, *who to be.* But two seconds after she rolls into Braemer, she's floundering, wondering if she ever really had an identity and, if so, where the hell she'd left it.

The phone leered at her. Calling Paris would be like admitting she didn't have a grip here. She nibbled on her lower lip, then pushed herself up and meandered to the far side of the room to peer into the trash. Too bad, the Ben & Jerry's was seriously melted.

But at least Mrs. Kelley hadn't cleaned the room. The I've-got-work-spread-across-the-floor story must have worked.

Okay, enough was enough. She lunged for the phone, dialing Paris's number before she could convince herself to hang up.

"Hello?"

"It's all Garrett's fault," she blurted.

"Hi, Rachel—" said a male voice.

Groaning, she banged the back of her head against the wall.

"—I'll get Paris."

"Thanks, Devin." Well, she shouldn't be too embarrassed. He already knew she was a nutcase.

From her end, she could hear Devin calling, "Rachel says it's Garrett's fault," and then the shuffle as the phone changed hands.

"Tell me."

And so she did. *Everything.* Even her entire sordid, clever, brilliant, stupid plan.

"I can't believe you slept with the wrong MacLean."

Rachel rolled her eyes. "That's old news. What do I do now?"

"Don't you just hate a considerate guy?" Paris's voice

faded as she repeated Rachel's comment about Garrett not wanting to pressure her.

"Doesn't want to pressure you means he's serious," Devin said, his voice loud and clear over the phone line.

"Devin!" Paris said. Then a couple of clunks and thunks as Paris wrestled the handset back. "Boy, you marry them and they think they know everything," she added, and Devin laughed in the background.

Rachel sighed, clutching her pillow to her chest and telling herself she wasn't jealous. Tracing a seam, she wondered how Garrett felt about pillow fights.

"Rach?"

"Sorry. I was looking at my pillows."

"Mmm," said Paris, as if she understood completely. "So he doesn't want to pressure you. That's cool. Chivalry is good."

"I suppose."

"Well, what do you want?" Paris asked reasonably.

Not chivalry. I want him to throw me down and make love to me until I break glass screaming. "I have no idea," she said. "I want him, okay?" So badly her body tingled with anticipation. So desperately she could taste it. She needed to finish what they started, and then some.

"So go to him."

"I don't know." She sighed. "Why him? Why now?" *Because he's safe.*

"Maybe he's The One. It's your turn, you know."

Rachel frowned, quashing the little voice in her head that suggested that maybe Paris was right. Maybe Garrett was more than safe, maybe he was special, too. The One. *Mr. Right.*

No way. Guys interested in meaningful relationships didn't agree to step aside so that the object of their affection could flirt with other guys. Everything he did and said made it crystal clear that he was looking for a temporary arrangement, no strings attached, nothing more than a good time.

But that made it all the more perfect, right? Because that's what she wanted, too. After all, her plan was still top priority. So a no-strings, great-sex deal with Garrett made perfect sense. She'd have no distractions, nothing to divert her from her plan. And that was good, because it was exactly what she wanted. *Really.*

"Rachel? Are you there?"

She sighed, her decision made. Then she remembered Garrett's instructions. "What do Tony Orlando and Dawn have to do with my sex life?"

The phone was silent, then Devin came on. "If we tell you are you going to do it?"

Rachel pressed her lips together, gathering her courage. It wasn't that much of a risk, right? No commitment, so she'd only be showing a little piece of her heart. And just because Carl had screwed her over didn't mean Garrett would, too.

"Yes," she finally said. "I promise."

FIFITY-EIGHT LITTLE ceiling tiles lined the length of Garrett's room, and thirty-two lined the width. He knew, because he'd counted them five times, and come up with the same number each time.

Frustrated, he twirled an unlit cigarette between his fingers. It had been over an hour since he'd left her room, and the scope and enormity of his stupidity had pretty much sunk in. *He'd blown it. She wasn't coming.*

Which meant he'd have to live up to his agreement to schlep her around town, watching her flirt with those creeps, all the while wanting her in his bed and knowing it wasn't going to happen.

Maybe he should regroup, go downstairs and—
Bang!

The sound echoed through the room and Garrett sat up, waiting for the rest of the message. Nothing. Damn. He slipped off the bed and pressed his ear to the floor. Eternity stretched out for a few more seconds. No more noise. Surely he hadn't imagined it.

Had she changed her mind? The thought depressed him.

Bang, bang, bang! His ear rang as the floor beneath him shook with the pounding, and Garrett was on his feet and at the door before the sound faded.

He took the stairs at a sprint, not bothering to stay quiet, then skidded to a stop in front of her door. It opened and there she was—beautiful and radiant and *wanting him.* "It's knock *three times* on the ceiling if you want me."

"I dropped the shoe." She grinned. "I didn't want you to misunderstand, so I started over."

His gaze roamed over her, his breath catching as he realized what she was wearing. "Love the scrubs."

She laughed. "I kept them." She opened the door wider and ushered him in. "I hope you don't mind."

"I don't mind." He kicked the door closed. "Take them off."

One eyebrow raised. "Demanding, aren't you?"

He heard the tease in her voice, and aimed it right back at her. "Unless you'd rather I just go back to my room?"

A beat, then she loosened the drawstring on the pants. The ugly green material grazed over her naked hips, down her firm thighs, to pool at her feet. He groaned, his body burning, his erection straining against his jeans. The scrub top hung just low enough to conceal, enticing

him with the possibilities that lay beyond that neckline.
Reaching out, he stroked her smooth skin there, taking
immense satisfaction in the rise and fall of her chest as
she tried to control her breathing.

"Why did you ask me back?"

"Why do you think?"

"Maybe you want to play truth or dare?" he said, his
voice low and teasing.

She nibbled on her lower lip.

He stepped closer, grazing his finger up her thigh, his
arm around her waist to keep her steady. She arched her
back against his hand, and he accepted the silent invitation, dipping down to kiss the soft skin peeking out from
the V-neck of the scrub top. "Truth," he murmured
against her skin.

"Guess," she answered, her voice breathy.

He wanted to tease, to torment, to make her desperate
for him. But he also wanted to know the answer. He
wanted to know she was his. Hell, he just *wanted*.

"You want me," he said, pitching his voice low. "Tell
me."

"I want you."

His breath came faster and his blood burned. She
sighed, her flesh so hot he could feel her desire through
his clothes.

He cupped her sweet rear, easing his finger lower as
her breath came anything but easy against his ear. She
moaned and sighed and squirmed against him, and he
teased her, his finger tracing her soft skin, testing the
sensitive area between her thighs and finally, *oh, God,
yes*, dipping inside her as she gasped and shivered in his
arms.

"You're wet," he murmured, and she nodded as her
mouth found his.

"Kiss me," she demanded, her lips brushing against his. "Make love to me."

He closed his mouth over hers, tasting her, drawing her deeper and deeper into him, until his body was on fire and he wondered how he could survive another minute of not being inside her. Reluctantly, he broke their kiss, taking her hips in his hands and turning her around, then pulling her close so that her rear pressed against him.

With a low groan, he slid his hands up until he cupped her breasts. She writhed against him, the soft pressure of her rear against his arousal threatening to undo him. With his thumb, he stroked her taut nipples.

"Garrett, please."

"Please what?" he whispered against her hair. "Tell me what you want. I want to hear it."

"I want you. I told you."

"So you said." The answer warmed and filled him, but it wasn't enough. He wanted *her*, exposed and real and desperate for him. Mata Hari could wait outside the door.

Moving them together, he urged her toward the bed, stroking her shoulders and then the curve of her back as he eased her onto the mattress, her back still to him. He peeled off his jeans and underwear, only then realizing that he'd run down to her room in bare feet.

"Garrett," she murmured, "I think we need that twenty-four hour pharmacy."

"Never fear, sweetheart." His feet might be bare, but fortunately, he'd had the presence of mind to stuff vital necessities into his back pocket. After a bit of rummaging, he joined her on the bed with a couple of little foil packets. "Ta-da."

She grinned. "My hero."

She took a packet and worked wonders, while he struggled for control, then she lay back on her stomach. Taking a deep breath, he leaned over her, his face near her neck, his erection buried between her thighs, just high enough and hard enough to tease her. "Now where were we?"

He moved against her and she moaned. "Right about here, I think."

"Tell me," he urged. "Tell me what you want."

"I want to finish what we started," she said. "Please, Garrett, *now*."

He urged her thighs apart, his pulse quickening as she shifted to open herself wider for him. *She wanted him.* Unable to hold back, he slid into her, just enough to drive them both crazy. "This?" he said, his voice raspy. "Is this what you want?"

"No...yes...all of you, Garrett, *please*."

He couldn't take any more, and he rolled her over, then thrust deep into her as her legs closed around his waist, urging him deeper and deeper. He leaned forward, pushing her shirt up until she yanked it over her head. He claimed her breast with his mouth as he lost himself in her silky sweetness.

"Oh, yes." She moaned and her fingers twined in his hair, urging him up, pulling his mouth to hers.

"Tell me who you are," he murmured. "Tell me who I'm with."

She thrust her hips up, forcing him deeper, and he groaned and wondered if it mattered who she was. *It did.* "Tell me," he said, then trailed kisses down the side of her face.

"I don't understand." But he didn't believe her.

"I want to be with you, with *Rachel*."

She stroked his back, every nerve ending in his body telling him to shut up and take her.

"You are," she said.

His body balanced on the edge, near to exploding, the world threatening to split into a million pieces as he claimed her, deep and hard. But he wanted to make sure she never again tried to hide from him.

He thrust deeper, watching her face, wide and open with passion. "The real Rachel," he added, forcing the words out. "I want the real woman, the one I saw in the clinic. Not the woman who's playing at seduction. Not Mata Hari."

"Mata Hari," she repeated, smiling as if they shared a joke.

"You, Rachel."

"You've got me." Her hands slid down, cupping his butt. She pulled him into her, thrusting her hips toward him as her hands pushed him deeper and deeper. "Now, Garrett. Please, *now.*"

Her answer washed over him, sweet and honest and enticing. She was real, she was his, and nothing else mattered.

HE WANTED HER.

She was on fire. Every atom in her body spinning, neurons firing, passion exploding.

He really wanted her. Miraculous. Amazing. And the world had never seemed so open, so full of light, so full of promise. He filled her, deeper and deeper, moving in a timeless rhythm, sending her to dizzying heights.

Someone was crying out, and she realized it was her.

When she opened her eyes several long moments later, he smiled at her. "Hey."

Pulling him close, she kissed him, long and deep, before falling back against the pillow, loving the feel of him on top of her and inside her.

"Hey yourself." She trailed her finger down his back, her brow furrowing as she realized what was wrong. "How do you always manage to stay dressed?"

"Dressed?"

She plucked at his T-shirt.

A slow grin played across his face. "I was in a hurry."

"Felt nice and slow to me," she said, then kissed him, remembering just how nice it had been. Better than nice. Hell, better than chocolate. Damn near perfect, actually.

"Well," she said with a frown, "I guess you're just going to have to try again until you get this right."

"Oh, yeah?"

She nodded, fighting a grin. Her hand slipped under the shirt and she stroked his skin.

He groaned, getting hard inside her again, filling her up.

"I think you've got real potential," she said. "No sense sluffing off now when you're so close to an A-plus."

"No sense at all," he agreed, reaching over his head and grabbing the back of his shirt. He hauled it off and threw it on the floor. "Let's see if I can't make the Dean's list."

She rolled her eyes at his pun, but amusement morphed into passion when he lowered his mouth to her breast, his breath hot and moist on her sensitive nipple. Then he shifted, pulling out of her, and she cried out in protest.

"Sshh," he murmured.

"That's not the way to up your grades." But then his mouth was on her stomach, then her navel, then lower still. Her body tightened in anticipation, craving release, yet wanting the moment to go on forever.

"Star pupil," she said when she remembered to breathe.

His silence spoke volumes, as his lips traveled lower still, teasing and tempting. The stubble of his beard brushed the insides of her thighs, his tongue delivering sweet torment until she cried out, then dipping inside to taste her secrets.

Shameless, she writhed against him, needing to feel his skin against hers, to know he was right there, and she ran her fingers down her belly, following the trail he'd blazed. Her fingers twined through his hair and she urged him higher. "Kiss me."

He smiled, his eyes dark with passion. "Just a kiss?"

So much more. She shook her head. "Figure out what I want now, and you'll get a scholarship," she said, dreamily. Then he quickly rolled on a fresh condom and straddled her. She closed her eyes, losing herself to his touch and knowing he'd figured it out.

As he thrust deep inside, she rose up, crying out as her body melted into stardust.

"Rachel," he whispered, his voice little more than a breath. When he pulled the tangled sheet from the foot of the bed, she snuggled against him, and he tucked the sheet around them, drawing her even closer to his body.

As his breathing evened, she twisted in his arms to watch his face, wanting to see him satisfied and sleepy. Through drooping eyes, he caught her gaze and smiled. "I think I deserve a *full* scholarship," he said.

She couldn't argue with that.

He drifted off, and she relaxed in his arms. For the moment at least, she was safe, cherished. She snuggled closer, wanting the moment to last, trying to hold the doubts and fears at bay. He'd said he wanted her, really wanted *her*. The idea that someone wanted the real Rachel—that was everything she'd always hoped.

Except...

As the heat of the moment faded, reality moved back in, ready to put a quick end to her silly delusions. Tugging the sheet up under her chin, she recalled his words. He said he wanted the Rachel he'd met in the clinic. But that wasn't her, not really. She'd been playing at seduction. So how could she show him the real Rachel? Especially since she didn't even know who that was anymore.

But she intended to find out. She'd come back to Braemer to find herself, and she wasn't about to abandon her plan. She gazed at the man dozing beside her. She wanted him so intensely her body quivered with desire. And she needed him to want her. The real her.

That made Garrett one more reason she had to finish what she started. And he'd promised to help her.

She snuggled under the sheet, pressing closer to his warmth. For now she was safe in his arms. Tomorrow, they'd find Jason or Derek.

THE MORNING SUN streamed through the French doors, and Garrett looked at the sleeping woman next to him, realizing that somewhere along the line he'd lost his heart. It was as though he was the director of a movie that had gone out of his control. He'd welcomed her into his arms hoping to keep her occupied, wanting to show her just how much he enjoyed her so that maybe she'd abandon her harebrained scheme. But he hadn't thought about the last reel, the ending that would send him back to California and Rachel back to New York, her self-esteem repaired and a few luscious memories in her suitcase.

He frowned, wondering if that ending would play in Peoria, because it sure didn't sit well with him.

Rolling on his side, he spooned against her, his heart about to burst when she pressed back against him, her body seeking his even in sleep. He kissed her shoulder, wondering when his subconscious had decided that Rachel was worth keeping around, worth fighting for.

No matter how you sliced it, Rachel was a complication. But there were good complications and bad ones. A complication during surgery was bad. A Rachel complication was good.

All the more so because she was *his* complication. Now all he needed was to convince her, too.

He kissed her ear and she rolled over, her breasts pressing against him, the sweet pressure wiping away the last remnants of sleep as his body buzzed to life.

Thumper whined and jumped off the foot of the bed, where he'd been curled up since Rachel had let him out of the bathroom. *Good dog.*

Lazily, her hands stroked him, making him hard, making him want her all over again.

"Take me," she whispered.

Garrett wasn't about to argue, and he lost himself in her arms, in her warmth, until he finally exploded inside her, sated and happy and certain that this was the woman for him.

"We have to leave the bed sometime," he said later. His feet were resting against the headboard, the sheets somewhere on the floor. Her body curled against his, and he dragged his hand lazily over her, teasing her nipples, relishing the knowledge that he could touch her anywhere, that she wanted his touch.

He snaked his hand down, his fingers seeking her heat.

"If you want to leave this bed, you'd better stop that," she said, but she didn't sound like she meant it.

She was still wet and swollen, and he stroked her, loving the way her body tensed against him as he brought her to the edge once again. She writhed against him, but he pulled away to trace lazy circles on the inside of her thighs.

She moaned in protest. "No fair."

"Not fair at all," he agreed, easing her over his thigh so he could slide off the bed. "But I'm covering all bases."

She smiled. "Come again?"

"I'm seriously considering that," he said with a grin.

"You're bad," she said, rolling her eyes. "What did you mean by bases?"

"I'm making sure that later today you want to finish what I just started." He grinned. "So far that's been a pretty good technique for getting you in my bed."

"You bum." She laughed, then hauled her pillow up and whonked him on the head. He ducked and managed to get her back, then he launched himself at her and trapped her under him, tickling her waist.

"Stop! Stop it. I'm too ticklish."

"Yeah? Well, you should have thought of that before you walloped me."

"Help, help," she squeaked between laughter, and then help was there—Thumper, with his paws on the edge of the bed, barking his head off.

"Mrs. Kelley'll hear him—"

"Hey, Thumper," he said, reaching a hand down to calm the dog. "Keep a lid on it, okay?"

"He probably needs a walk."

"Then we really should get up," he said, glancing toward the clock. "It's morning."

"The clinic?"

"That and food," he said. "We need to keep up our strength."

Nodding, she sat up, pulling the sheet around her. "We sure do. I don't want to risk you going all weak in the knees on me." Her mouth twitched. "Or any other parts for that matter."

"No risk of that." He let his gaze roam her body, naked under that one thin sheet. "No risk at all."

"Good." She sat up. "So what's on our agenda?"

"After the clinic I thought I'd pick you up and we'd grab a late lunch, then maybe drive around. I haven't seen Braemer or the rest of the county in years, and I figure you haven't either. And since we've already done the dancing thing, I thought maybe tonight we'd take in a movie." He smiled, imagining sharing a bucket of popcorn and watching a Hitchcock retrospective. "We could rent something if there's nothing good playing in Braemer."

"Quite an itinerary."

"Do you approve?"

"Oh, yeah," she said, her tone leaving no doubt she thought it was a hell of a plan. "Except for that part about picking me up. I'm going with you."

"Four hours in the clinic? You'll be bored stiff."

"So I'll help. I can play receptionist," she said, then winked. "I'm multitalented. Trust me. I'll be useful." She shrugged. "Worst case, I'll end up playing solitaire on the computer."

What the hell. If she wanted to tag along he wasn't inclined to discourage her. "Sounds like a plan."

He'd spend the next few days wining and dining her,

and showing her a hell of a time in the Texas Hill Country. Not only did that mean he got to spend that much more time with her, but it meant that—right up to the reunion—she'd be with him and not out putting the moves on Jason or Derek.

She slid off the bed, pulling the sheet around her like a toga as she padded toward the bathroom, and looking so adorable he almost forgot that they needed to get a move on.

At the doorway, she paused and looked back at him. "Don't forget your promise," she said, and Garrett wondered if he'd popped that mental champagne a little too early. "Sometime today you have to take me out on the town. We need to meet up with Jason and Derek."

Garrett sighed and ran his hands through his hair. *Damn.*

11

RACHEL PLASTERED on her most polite smile and bit back a howl of frustration.

Across the reception counter, Scott Carter struggled to keep a firm grip on a slippery beagle named Snoopers. "I still can't believe I recognized you," he said. "You look great." Giving up, he shifted his attention to Snoopers, trying to convince the dog that being at the vet's wasn't the worst thing in the world.

In her head, Rachel let out a long-suffering sigh. She still couldn't believe he'd recognized her either. She'd been fighting with the clinic's ancient computer when he'd come in, done a double-take, then guffawed and smiled broadly.

Didn't that just suck? She'd changed so much, yet it had only taken him an instant to see Belinda Rachel. Even more annoying, if she hadn't seen his name on the schedule, she'd never have recognized him.

Not for the first time, a twinge of uncertainty crept up her neck. What if the Stooges recognized her, too? Maybe she should just forget about her plan and go back to New York.

She pushed the thought away. Scott was just a fluke. She'd seen Jason last night, after all, and he'd been clueless.

Besides, going back to Manhattan would mean leaving Garrett. Right now, the idea was unthinkable.

Scott gave up trying to control the writhing mass and put the dog down, then he belatedly stuck out a hand and waited for her to take it. "Belinda Dean. Wow. We had no idea what planet you'd disappeared to."

"Manhattan," she said. After a couple of vigorous pumps he let go. He propped an elbow on the counter as Snoopers snuffled around the waiting area, checking out the linoleum.

"So, you came back for the reunion, huh?"

Behind the counter, Rachel nodded, figuring that was pretty close to the truth.

"I'm glad. A lot of folks wondered where you'd gone off to."

A lot of folks?

"Someone heard you'd gone to law school," he added. "Didn't surprise me, what with you always having your nose in a book."

She nodded vaguely, still overwhelmed that *a lot of folks* had wondered about her. Her eyes misted and she blinked.

"I'm glad," he went on. "That was a real shitty stunt Jason pulled at the prom."

"Yes, it was." She said it matter-of-factly, awed by the realization that she hadn't been completely invisible.

The examining room door opened and Garrett's stepmother stuck her head out. "Okay, Scott. You and Snoopers can come on back. Garrett'll be in just as soon as he finishes in the O.R."

"Scott," Rachel called, and he paused in front of the examining room. "Thanks," she said, her voice shaky. She was *not* going to cry.

"See you at the dance. Save me one, okay?" he said, then coaxed Snoopers through the door.

Rachel watched him disappear, her lower lip trembling.

Jennie glanced at Rachel and smiled. "You doing okay, hon?"

"Sure," she lied, quashing the urge to tell everything, to confide her entire plan to the sweet, motherly woman. Since Jennie was asking about how Rachel was handling the receptionist role—not about the state of her mental health—spilling her guts probably wasn't a good idea.

"I'm fine," she added, then focused on the computer until Jennie nodded and followed Scott into the little room.

She was not going to cry. Was not, was not, was not.

A tear trickled down her cheek and she wiped it away, sniffing. So much for mind over matter.

THE LUSH GREEN TONES of the Texas Hill Country drifted by as Garrett aimed the truck down the highway. Next to him, Rachel had settled in, lost among bags and boxes.

He'd promised her a run-in with Derek later this afternoon after he got off work, and she'd dressed for the upcoming part—sexy sandals that showed off her painted toenails, silky walking shorts that clung just enough when she moved, and a summer sweater that accentuated her curves. She looked classy and sexy and beautiful. If she turned up the heat, Derek would be a goner.

Hell, Garrett already was. And the thought of any other man looking at her *that way* ate at his gut.

She caught him eyeing her and smiled. "What?"

"Can't I look at the woman I'm sharing my truck with?"

She blushed and avoided the question. "Thanks for

this outing," she countered. "I had loads of fun. I hadn't been to Fredericksburg in ages."

He hid a smile, happy to know he was rolling down the highway with the real Rachel—the one who blushed and laughed. She'd probably shift into seduction mode soon enough, but for now she was all his.

She rummaged in a bag and came up with a hand-carved wooden troll. "Isn't he just the ugliest thing you ever saw?"

Garrett grinned and agreed. The troll was hideous. But the old German immigrant who'd sold it to Rachel had been fascinating, telling them stories about the early days in Texas as he'd shared kolaches and coffee.

"Now what are you smiling about?"

"Am I?" he asked. He held out a hand and she pushed the bags out of her way as she slid over next to him. "I guess that old man brought home how much I miss a laid-back lifestyle," he said. "In L.A., everything's rush, rush, rush."

"Mmmm-hmmm." She nodded, leaning her head against his shoulder and closing her eyes. "New York, too," she said, sounding sleepy and satisfied.

His mood switched to melancholy as he remembered that she wouldn't be staying in Braemer. He frowned. *Neither would he.*

A couple of days enjoying the lifestyle didn't mean he should pack up and move back. After all, he'd made a mint catering to celebrities with exotic pets. But that was more baby-sitting than anything else. Before he'd helped birth that foal, it'd been years since he'd felt any real exhilaration. Or even the sense of community that came with the day-to-day practice of a small-town vet. Like this morning. His fourth grade teacher had actually brought him cookies. Homemade sugar cookies with those ridiculous colored sprinkles.

The fattest bank account in the world couldn't buy that feeling. It was priceless.

Rachel shifted, and he realized she'd fallen asleep. Not too surprising considering they'd been awake most of the night. He smiled, remembering the reason for their shared exhaustion.

Mindlessly, his fingers grazed her bare leg, just above her knee. The real truth was, he'd been toying more and more with the idea of staying, of working in the clinic like Jennie and Carl seemed to want. But staying would mean sitting down with his dad and talking—*really talking*. Something they hadn't done in close to eighteen years. If he suggested staying to his father—and if the old man rejected him again—well, that was something Garrett wasn't sure he could stomach.

If he kept silent, though, he still had a fighting chance. He could tell himself that Jennie and Carl were right, that his father did want him here.

But if he made the overture...if his father said no...

Then all bets were off.

Disgusted with himself, he slammed his palm against the steering wheel, then immediately looked down to make sure he hadn't woken Rachel. Her eyes were still closed, her lips slightly parted. In her hand, she held the troll. Hardly the epitome of a femme fatale.

He smiled. Her plan was insane, but that was one of the things he loved about her—she didn't shun the unexpected and she went after what she wanted.

Loved. With a frown, he tapped the brakes, automatically slowing as reality blindsided him. There it was again—*love*—and this time he didn't try to deny it. He wasn't sure when it happened, but somehow he knew with absolute certainty that Rachel—along with all her incarnations—was the only woman for him.

With a low chuckle, he reached over to take her hand. Her fingers closed around his, but she didn't wake up.

As much as he thought her plan was absurd, he had to hand it to her. At least she was out there confronting her demons. It was a bizarre little plan—and one that he intended to bring to a screeching halt—but at least she was trying.

Well, if she could do it, so could he. And despite all his denials, despite telling himself for years that it didn't matter what his dad thought, the truth was that he wanted—no, *needed*—to know if his father had really wanted him to come.

He relaxed as they neared the Austin city limits, sure that he'd finally made the right decision. Hell, just *deciding* was cathartic. Imagine how he'd feel if Jennie and Carl were right.

He pushed the thought aside. No sense getting his hopes up.

And in the meantime, until he talked to his dad, there was still one more thing he wanted. *Rachel.*

As if he'd said the words aloud, she shifted, turning to look up at him. "Are we going to find Derek now?"

Garrett glanced at his watch. Derek wouldn't be at the park for at least another two hours. He'd told Rachel a little white lie, and he hoped it paid off.

"Pretty soon," he said.

They were going to Austin to see Derek, but he didn't really live there, only drove in once a week. But Garrett doubted she'd figure that out. And if she did, why be mad? After all, he was taking her to him, so *technically* he was fulfilling his part of the bargain. Of course, he did have an ulterior motive.

Everyone Garrett had talked to had been unanimous. As Elmer at the gas station put it, "the bad seed grew up into a right solid tree." But it hadn't been until he was about to give Snoopers a cortisone shot that Garrett learned about Derek's weekly picnic for troubled kids enrolled in an outreach program. Thanks to Scott Carter, Garrett's plan had really gelled.

Jason might be a lost cause, but Derek was practically the poster boy for reformed souls. So for Garrett's purposes anyway, Rachel couldn't have set her sights on a better former jerk. And from what he could tell, *former* really was the operative word.

Already he could tell she was warming up to Braemer, finally seeing it in a new light. He just needed to take her that last baby step. Let her see that the folks she knew from high school—most of them anyway—had changed. Then maybe she'd realize that she'd changed, too.

She yawned. "Well, where are we going now?"

"It's a surprise."

"Sounds dangerous."

He traced his fingers higher, under the hem of her shorts, the silky material grazing the back of his hand. "This kind of dangerous?"

He heard her breath catch. "We're on the highway."

"So we are." A quick glance in his rearview mirror confirmed that no one was behind them. "Whenever and however I want, remember?"

She twisted in her seat and quirked a brow. "Hold on a second there, buster," she said, her smile destroying the illusion that she was irritated. "That was the old deal. You walked away. I distinctly remember *that*."

"Well, you've got a point," he said, but didn't stop. Instead, he flattened his palm on her thigh and stroked, higher and higher until his fingers grazed the edge of her panties.

Rachel held her breath, fighting the urge to move just enough, wanting him to touch her there, to touch her everywhere. No matter what he said, this *was* dangerous. Not because they were going to crash into another car on the near-empty highway, but because her heart was on some sort of wild ride. She'd never been as open, never had as much fun, with a man as she'd had with Garrett, and the realization terrified and excited her.

He took his eyes off the road for just an instant. "I guess that means you're in charge of whenever and however." The corner of his mouth curled as his fingers sent waves of sensations through her body.

His hand, rough against her skin, was like a talisman, leaving her warm and supple in its wake. His finger teased her, slipping intimately under her panties, teasing secret places, until she knew she was wet and wanted to scream for him to just pull the truck over and take her right then, right there.

"When and how, Rachel," he repeated, as if reading her mind. "You tell me."

She licked her lips, reveling in the sweet sensations of his fingers stroking her, fanning flames that threatened to consume her. While part of her wanted to continue, another part knew that the deeper she fell, the harder it would be to walk away from Braemer when their time was over. Oh, God, it didn't matter anyway. Already, she was in deep. Already, it would be hell leaving.

And if that hell was already waiting around the corner, she might as well take what she wanted now—*Garrett*.

"Here," she said, her voice breathy with need. "And now."

His finger slipped higher, closer, almost *there*, and she squirmed trying to bring him closer, higher, deeper.

"Right here?" he murmured.

Oh, yes. He touched her, stroking and caressing, faster then slower until she couldn't stand it any longer and her body tensed, on the verge of snapping back, a vibrato alive with energy and yet craving more.

"Oh, Garrett..." She opened her eyes, wanting to see his face, but only seeing his taut profile, as he kept his eyes on the road and his hand on her, his thumb dancing over her most sensitive spot, bringing her closer until she threatened to explode. She shut her eyes. "Please..."

"Sweetheart," he said, his voice rough, "I think it's high time I pulled over."

RACHEL STRETCHED, sleepy and satisfied. Two decadent hours in a hotel with Garrett had just about done her in. But now they were in Austin. Just as he'd promised, he was helping with her plan. And that meant it was time to turn on the charm for Derek.

When he turned into Zilker Park, she twisted in her seat to face him again. "We're going to the park?"

"We're going right there," he said, pointing to a picnic area filled with boisterous preteens.

That didn't make sense. The park was great, but she didn't see what it had to do with Derek—unless he was now Dumpster-diving after school picnics. Most likely she wouldn't be that lucky. Rich creeps tended to remain rich creeps. She'd picked up on that about two seconds after seeing Jason again.

She glanced over at Garrett. Maybe he wasn't keeping his promise after all. She bit the inside of her cheek, wondering if she should insist on tracking down Derek, or just go with whatever Garrett had in mind for them.

Maybe another romantic interlude. She smiled, the possibility cheering her.

"Derek should be just over that way," he said, and she measured the disappointment gathering in her chest.

Garrett lucked into a parking space, and they headed back, holding hands as they walked. The sidewalk ran the length of the fenced-off pool, and the main building hid them from the view of anyone in the picnic area. As they stepped into the open, Garrett swung his arm around her, and pulled her close.

"Show time," he said, looking sincere and helpful. "Right?"

Nodding, she steeled herself, trying not to be ticked he was pushing her toward Derek even though he knew she planned to flirt like mad. *That was the idea, remember?* He was *supposed* to be sincere and helpful. Arm candy. Lord knows she needed the props lately. Switching into seductress mode was getting more and more difficult. New York Rachel kept packing up to go shopping. At this rate, her closet was going to be filled to overflowing.

The howls and laughter from the picnic area got louder as they neared. "Do you see him?" Garrett asked.

She shook her head, then heard a voice— "Tony, how many times do I have to tell you not to pick on the littler kids?"

Derek.

She sucked in air, suddenly certain she didn't want to flirt, didn't want to prove anything to anybody. She just wanted to go home and hide under the covers until she got her head back on straight. She blinked back tears, not knowing where home was anymore.

"Derek Booker?" Garrett called. "Man, it sure is a coincidence running into you here."

Rachel bit back a laugh. An actor, Garrett wasn't.

Derek looked up from the merry-go-round he was pushing and squinted in their direction as Garrett steered them onward, his arm still firm around her shoulder.

Derek paused, then pointed, a genuine smile spreading across his jovial face. "Garrett MacLean! How the heck are you? I haven't seen you in ages. Why are you in Austin?"

Garrett took his arm off Rachel long enough to shake Derek's hand. "Visiting Braemer. Thought I'd do the tourist thing." He nodded at Rachel. "This is my friend Rachel. Rachel, Derek Booker."

She shook his hand, trying not to be depressed by the *friend* label. What else could he have said? Lover? Girlfriend? Neurotic sidekick?

Physically, Derek hadn't changed much. He was still a big guy, and his *Just Say No To Drugs* T-shirt fit a little too snug. But while she'd remembered him as cold, the man in the park seemed warm and friendly.

"Rachel," he said. "The names's not familiar, but something about you is. Have we met?"

She was saved from answering when two boys wrestled to a stop beside him. Derek managed to untangle them, figure out what started the fight, and soothe hurt feelings—all without breaking a sweat.

When he'd sent the boys on their way, he flashed an apologetic smile toward Rachel and Garrett. "They're a handful sometimes, but you should have seen them two months ago when we started this program."

Rachel wasn't sure what he meant. "Program?"

He puffed up, clearly proud of whatever he had going here. "It's a state-sponsored project. We take troubled kids and try to give them some adult support. The idea is to straighten them out before they get to high school."

How ironic that a guy like Derek would work on a project like that. "How'd you get involved?"

"Well, it was my idea."

"Oh," she said, then realized she'd taken an involuntary step backwards. "Why?"

Garrett saved her from looking like a total idiot by pulling her closer. Thankful that he understood how much Derek's statement had shaken her, she leaned into him.

"It's important for these kids to have a network so they don't get sucked in by peer pressure." He laughed mirthlessly. "Garrett can tell you, I was hell on wheels in school. Did a lot of things I regret to a lot of people. So I know from experience how important a program like this is."

"Right," Rachel said, not sure what else to say. Holding her, Garrett trailed his fingers up and down her arm, the touch teasing and exciting her, even though she knew that right then he was playing the role they'd written—*constantly and affectionately.*

Except now, flirting with Derek seemed ludicrous. Once again, she'd been knocked off kilter, stuck in a mission that kept experiencing critical failures along the way. And now she didn't know if she should regroup and start over, or hit the abort button and make the whole thing go away.

Whatever she decided, right then she needed out of there.

"It was nice to meet you, Derek." She looked up at Garrett. "Don't we need to head back to Braemer?"

She saw confusion, then what looked like victory in his eyes. "Didn't you want to stay in Austin for a while?"

"No." She looked to Derek and then back to Garrett. "There's nothing here I need to do."

He smiled at her. "Well, then let's go home."

12

ANABEL'S HAD BEEN the favorite Braemer eatery since before Rachel was born, and from the noise level that assaulted them as they walked through the door, she figured it wasn't going out of business anytime soon.

Garrett steered them to the same booth they'd had the night before. Then, just before closing, the place had been dead. Now, it was buzzing with adults and kids out for a family dinner. A waitress sidled over, and Rachel looked up, surprised to see Lucy.

"Well, if it isn't dancing Rachel. How you doing, sugar?"

"I'm good," she said, meaning it. She nodded toward Garrett and they shared a secret smile. "This is Garrett."

"I'm sure it is," Lucy said, eyeing him. "What are you kids having, besides a good time?"

Garrett reached across the booth to grab her hand. "A grilled chicken salad and a Diet Coke for the lady," he said, pausing to give her a chance to change the order. She just raised an eyebrow in approval and took a sip of water. "And a double cheeseburger, large fries and a chocolate shake for me."

Lucy put a hand on her hip and flashed a jaunty look. "You should take lessons from the lady, or you're not always going to look so fine, and she won't put up with you."

Rachel choked on her water, then burst out laughing

while Garrett put on a face that was probably supposed to look offended, but really just looked amused.

"Is that right, Rach?" His eyes met hers and the corner of his mouth curved up, leaving her unsure exactly what he was asking.

Yes, he looked fine. And the truth was, his looks might fade. But even if they did, she'd always put up with him.

The realization disturbed her, because there was no always. In just a couple of days, she'd return to New York, and he'd head back to California. She'd come to Braemer hoping to find herself, and instead she'd found Garrett. Wonderful Garrett.

She should be thrilled, exuberant. Instead, she couldn't shake the thin sheen of melancholy that clung to her. As much as she cherished Garrett, he didn't know the real Rachel. He didn't know the woman behind the mask. Not really.

How could he? Hell, Rachel still didn't know that woman, and now she was more confused than ever.

Lucy slid some silverware and a bottle of ketchup onto the table. "I'll be back with your drinks in a bit," she said, taking their menus.

"I used to come here every day after school," Garrett said after she'd gone. "I'd stay for an hour and do my homework, then go work at the clinic."

"I never hung out here," Rachel admitted. "This is where my mom worked nights." She shrugged, trying to dismiss the memory. All those years, she'd been so lonely, and she'd felt guilty for feeling that way. After all, her mother had worked her butt off to make a home for them. But all Rachel had really wanted was more time with her mother.

She sat up straighter, determined not to be sucked under by memories. "Anyway, I like it here now," she said, surprising herself, but realizing that she meant it.

Lucy came back with their drinks and nodded toward the far side of the room, behind Rachel. "Looks like you two've got an audience."

Garrett frowned, and Rachel twisted in her seat to see what he was looking at.

Jason. Oh, hell.

When she saw his eyes widen with recognition, she spun back around to face Garrett.

"Jason," she said, stupidly. Her next victim on a silver platter. She watched as Garrett's jaw clenched and his face tightened, and she realized she wasn't interested in flirting with Jason, not tonight anyway. Maybe not ever.

Before she could find the words, Garrett gave a tight nod and moved to her side of the booth, his nearness comforting and reassuring. His fingers eased through her hair, sending sparks of awareness racing through her as he angled his mouth over hers. She drank in his taste, hot and masculine. She curled her toes in her sandals, trying to hold onto the sensation, trying to forget her doubts, wanting to memorize the tingly feeling spreading through her limbs and collecting deep within her.

There was safety in his arms. Contentment. It felt right. *Garrett* felt right. She took a deep breath and snuggled closer. So warm, so safe.

With a start, she realized that her enthusiasm for her original plan had truly fizzled. Now, the idea of seducing Jason—and revealing him as scum at the reunion dance—held no appeal at all. She'd come to Braemer with three seductions in mind, and now she only wanted one—a permanent one. But she wanted the whole package, and she had no clue where to start.

They'd gotten off on the wrong foot with their lies and deceits and crafty little plans. Now the right thing to do would be to tell him, let him know she wanted only him—and not just in bed—and see where that path led. Leaning closer, she opened her mouth, but he spoke first.

"Constantly and affectionately," he said, and reality slammed back with a thud.

An act.

Damn her for a fool, he was just acting a part. There was no path, there was no future. She'd let her guard down, and the truth had slapped her in the face.

She jerked away, her lips pressed tight together to stave off those damn tears. He'd wanted sex—they both had—and they'd gotten it in spades.

"Looks like it's show time," he whispered, and she cringed.

Idiot. She cursed herself for accepting his offer to play the affectionate boyfriend, cursed herself for making something out of nothing. Somewhere, she'd lost track of what was real and what was an act. As much as she might want a happily ever after with Garrett, there was no future there, just castles in the air. He wanted her in his bed, not in his life. He'd wanted a wild time with the tempting little seductress from the clinic. But that wasn't the real Rachel. And she'd done enough pretending for the decade.

She ignored the little voice telling her she was wrong—that Garrett was sincere. That little voice was dangerous, would lead to heartache and more shattered illusions. There were so many barriers between them, not the least of which was an entire continent. Besides, he'd never said anything about a future together, and she wasn't about to stake her heart on lust and a childish belief in happy endings. She'd been hurt too many times before to start believing now.

She needed to get away. Wanted to go back to her room and curl up with Thumper and a pint of Mrs. Kelley's secret stash. Being with Garrett was just going to break her heart.

"I need out," she said, and for a brief, wonderful moment, his face hardened, and she thought he would stop her. But then he slid out of the booth and let her pass.

"Break a leg," he said, and she shivered.

"If it isn't the little lady from the Cotton Gin," Jason said, leering up at her as she headed for the back door. "You left me high and dry the other night."

"And I'm leaving you again," she snapped, irritated that he'd stopped her, and even more irritated that he shared the same planet as her and Garrett.

"Feeling feisty?" He nodded toward the chair opposite him. "I like a feisty woman."

The lust in his eyes was unmistakable, and it hit her. She'd won. She'd really and truly won. Jason Stilwell wanted her.

And she didn't give a damn.

"Are you gonna sit down, or what?"

"No," she said, shaking her head. "I'm through with you, Jason Stilwell." Her eyes narrowed. "But thanks for the memories."

Then she spun on her heel and left, doubting he caught the sarcasm, but feeling proud of herself for throwing it out there.

"Follow me," she hissed at Lucy as she headed toward the back of the café. If she went back to their booth, her resolve would fade the minute she saw Garrett.

In the little alcove by the pay phones and rest rooms, she found a take-out menu and scribbled a note, then pressed it into Lucy's hand. "Can you give this to Garrett?"

"Sure thing. You two kids have a fight? Not about Jason Stilwell, I hope. That man's a bastard."

Rachel agreed, but didn't bother to say so. "Not a fight, not really. I just..." She trailed off, unsure. She nodded toward the note. "We had this...arrangement. But it was stupid and I'm calling it off." Calling everything off.

She bit her lip, remembering they'd come in Garrett's truck. "I don't suppose Braemer has a taxi service?"

Lucy casually checked her watch. "Just call me Lucy's Yellow Cab." At Rachel's questioning glance, she shrugged. "No big deal. I'm done with my shift anyway."

GARRETT POUNDED ON Carl's front door, willing his little brother to be home. The gods must have been on his side—*it was about time*—because after a few seconds, the bolt clicked back, then the door opened.

"What the hell's wrong with you?" Carl said, and Garrett knew he must have looked as bad as he felt.

"Belinda Rachel Dean," he said, dragging himself inside.

"Aw, hell," Carl said. "You're not going to hit me again, are you?"

Garrett shook his head. "But if you can't help me figure out what to do, I just might."

"So what happened?"

Garrett related the Cliff's Notes version of their arrangement, while Carl's face reflected increasing incredulity as the story went on.

"That's the stupidest plan I ever heard. You were going to help her seduce Jason and Derek? What were you thinking?"

"I was thinking that I'd get to be with her, and that she'd realize her brilliantly devious plan wasn't so brilliant after all." He shrugged and passed Carl her note. "Looks like it worked, too. Unfortunately, it worked a little too well. My damn plan backfired when I played the lusting boyfriend role in front of Jason."

He slammed his fist into his palm of his hand. "Dammit! I just wanted to jolt her, to make her realize how absurd the whole thing was. I thought after Derek..." he trailed off, shaking his head. "Instead, I screwed up big time."

"Her *herring?*" Carl frowned, looking at her note. "A fish? What does she mean, *The deal's off. You don't have to be my herring anymore?*"

"Private joke. It means I've been fired from the resident love-interest position."

"I take it that's a position you're interested in keeping?"

"Damn right."

Carl's jaw clenched. "Going to be hard, with her in New York and you in California."

"I'm staying." He rolled the words over in his head, testing the decision. So far, no huge flashes of remorse.

Carl gaped. "Really?"

"Probably." He locked eyes with Carl, the great stare-off, waiting for Carl to break. One beat, then another. Carl just kept staring, until finally Garrett had to look away. Chalk one up for his baby brother.

"Probably?" Carl repeated, an edge to his voice.

"If what you and Jennie say is true."

A real smile spread across Carl's face. "Of course it's true."

"Need a project?" He'd been kicking the idea around. Might as well make the plunge.

Carl cocked his head. "Like what?"

"I'm interested in whether the old Duncan property is for sale."

"You *are* serious."

"Right now, I'm just planning ahead."

"Bullshit," Carl said.

Garrett answered with a shrug. A lot of things had to happen before Garrett would move back. He needed to sell his practice for one. But more than that, he needed to know his dad really wanted his help. Despite Carl's assurances, that was one loose end still dangling out there.

But first and foremost, he needed to get Rachel back. Somehow, he wasn't sure he could live in Braemer without her. Already, she'd permeated every nook and cranny, and he didn't think he could stand turning a corner and knowing he'd never see her around the next bend.

"I'm going to do everything I can to convince her to stay here. With me," Garrett said.

"Shouldn't be too hard."

"A lot you know. On top of everything else, the woman's got a law practice in New York."

"True, but I looked her up in Martindale's. She does a lot of appellate work, when she does legal stuff at all. Most of her business comes from her literary agency. Rachel can live wherever she wants."

"You've been busy."

"I've been nosy," Carl said.

But would she want to live in Braemer? After all, a few days of pleasure in the town might not make a dent in a lifetime of wanting out of it. But maybe she would. Under the right circumstances, and if all her demons where dead, then maybe.

And, come hell or high water, he'd figure out a way to convince her.

"My real problem is that I don't know how to convince her. I don't think she believes I could really want her. She has this whole seduction routine going, and she used it on you—well, me—that first night."

Carl cringed, but Garrett went on. "But there's a real woman under the act. Beautiful and funny and with a hell of a lot more confidence than she realizes, but she doesn't think anyone sees." With a sigh, he sat on the couch. "This is one man who not only saw her, but fell in love with her."

Carl's face crinkled with held-in laughter.

"What's so funny?" Irritated, he sat up and fished in his back pocket. No cigarettes. He'd thrown the damn things away.

"You," Carl finally said. "I've never seen you this passionate about a woman. It must really be love."

"It is," said Garrett simply. "I don't intend to let her get away."

Carl nodded, turning serious. "Good. She deserves to have a man fight for her. I should have beat the shit out of Derek and Jason years ago. If I had, maybe you'd be having an easier time of it now."

All true, but nothing they could do about it now. "Don't beat yourself up. It's the past, and it's done. I'm only concerned about here and now." *About Rachel.*

"So what are you going to do?"

Garrett shrugged. "Talk to her. Make her understand. Even if that means fighting that cement-cast self-doubt she's got going."

"Right now?"

"Hell, yes." He took a step toward the door.

Carl waved the note. "Do you think that's such a good idea? It sounds like she needs to calm down."

Garrett exhaled, fighting the urge to rush to her. Grudgingly, he admitted that Carl might be right. She probably did want some time to think. "You're right," he finally said, eyeing Carl's couch. "Can I crash here?"

"Sure. So when are you going to talk to her?"

"She said she'd help at the clinic tomorrow. I'll do it then." Besides, that would give him time to figure out what to say.

"You don't think she'll bail on you?"

"No, she promised Jennie. She's not the type to back out of a commitment."

As Carl went to grab some sheets for the couch, Garrett realized he'd hit upon his answer. His Rachel really wouldn't go back on her word. He was sure of that.

And she'd promised him that she'd let him see her. *All of her.*

Tomorrow, that was a promise he intended to see that she kept.

THUMPER WASN'T BEING any help at all. Rachel had walked him in the Bluebonnet's garden, and now, back in their room, he was just sitting like a loveable black lump on the quilt next to her, his tail whumping wildly, as she scratched behind his ears.

He was in doggie heaven, and she was in people hell.

"It's not fair," she said to him, and he opened his eyes and gave her a look that said, *you got yourself into this mess, I'm just along for the doggie-treats.*

"Well, you could at least try to help. I'm floundering here." Another understatement.

She dialed Paris's number, but the phone just rang

and rang. "Great." She looked at Thumper. "Couldn't they have waited until after my personal crisis?"

He yawned.

"I'm being neurotic, not selfish. There's a difference."

At that, he quivered all over, then stretched, presenting his belly for a rub. She complied, drawing some comfort from the fact that at least Thumper loved her unconditionally. Well, that brought the count up to two. Her best friend and her dog.

And Garrett.

She closed her eyes and fell back against the headboard. That was just wishful thinking. Garrett was a great guy, and maybe under different circumstances, they might have even had a chance, but she'd blown any real possibilities a week ago when she'd left New York with her mission on her mind.

He'd met her when she was in full-tilt sex kitten mode, and that image would forever color his perception.

"I just think it's a little much to hope that he'd want to give up a femme fatale for regular old me," she said to Thumper, who climbed to his feet and licked tears off her face. She hadn't even realized she'd been crying. Sniffing, she flung her arms around his neck. "Thanks, boy. I can always count on you."

Now she just wanted to get away. To go home and have a good cry in her apartment before the landlord kicked her out and she had to find a new place to live.

A knock on the door startled her, and she managed to grab Thumper's muzzle and muffle his bark. "Shhhh."

"Rachel?"

Mrs. Kelley. Damn. She looked at Thumper. "Bathroom. Now."

Thumper yawned and wagged his tail, but didn't move. Great.

"Just a sec. I gotta put something on." She shoved at the dog, who wasn't budging. She could pull all the bed-clothes off, and the dog along with them, but it was a long drop to the floor, and even if the fall didn't muck up his leg, he'd make a hell of a bang.

"Fine," she whispered. "You win. But *don't move.*" She tossed the bedspread over him, then took all of her clothes out of the bottom drawer and threw them in a pile on the lump. Not perfect, but so long as Thumper stayed quiet, it might work.

"Stay," she whispered again, going to the door.

Carrying a paper bag, Mrs. Kelley stopped in the doorway and glanced around the room. "You must be finished with your project."

"What?" Then she remembered the papers that were supposedly scattered across the floor. "Right. Just finishing up tonight, actually." She cleared her throat and eyed the bed, trying to decide if the pile of clothes looked like it was breathing. "What's up?"

"I thought maybe you needed an ear. You seemed a bit down when you came in. And I noticed that Garrett wasn't with you."

Rachel smiled. "You don't miss much."

"I have an excuse. I'm a nosy old woman." She gave Rachel a grandmotherly smile. "Do you want to talk about it?"

"No thanks." She glanced at the bed. Her confidantes were a dog and an absent best friend. "Maybe," she said, before she could change her mind.

"Did you two have a quarrel?"

"Not exactly." She paused, deciding what to say. "We're just not right for each other." That was half-true, anyway. Garrett was perfect for her, but she wasn't the woman he wanted.

"From what I've seen, I'd have to disagree."

Rachel smiled at that. Their time together had seemed perfect, and she intended to hang tight to her memories. She'd need them to get through the future alone. "The thing is," she admitted, "the way we met...he thinks I'm a certain kind of woman. That's who he wants, but that's not who I am."

Mrs. Kelley thought about that for a second. "For what it's worth, honey, I think you're wrong."

"Wrong?"

"I think Garrett sees more in you than you give him credit for." Still in the doorway, she held out the paper bag. "I brought you something."

Rachel took the bag as Mrs. Kelley winked. "A lot of people see more than you think," she added as she pulled the door shut.

She frowned, not sure what Mrs. Kelley meant. She headed back to the bed and shoved the laundry off Thumper. Then she peeled back the spread and crawled into bed.

A smile touched her lips when she finally peered into the bag.

One pint of Chunky Monkey.

And a plastic bag filled with doggie snacks.

13

RACHEL FROWNED at the computer, wondering if she'd ever get Mr. Bedford's invoice to print. She was tired and cranky and on edge because Garrett was about twenty feet away, with just a few walls between them. And as soon as he finished examining Tootsie, he'd walk through that door and she'd see him again.

Oh, Lord, she wanted to see him again. Wanted to touch him, to have him hold her and make it all better.

He hadn't come to her last night, and that only confirmed what she already knew. Their deal was off, so it was over. He didn't want her, he'd just wanted a fling.

She knew she needed to be strong. The problem was, she didn't want to be strong, if it meant being alone. She'd rather be weak and in his arms. And the printer was getting the brunt of her frustration. She walloped the top of the machine one more time. "Okay, now just print. It's easy. All the other computers do it. So can you."

"Don't fret it, honey. I can just write them up by hand," Jennie said.

"No," Rachel shook her head. She was on a mission now. "I spent hours yesterday setting this stuff up. It's the principle of the thing. Besides, you guys are still in the dark ages. Once we've got the computer up and running, things will be a lot easier."

Kneeling down, Jennie reorganized the pet food display. "I'm not very handy with computers, and neither is Carl." She looked up at Rachel. "My husband, I mean. Not my son."

Rachel nodded, still amazed that she could hang out and chat so easily with Carl's mother—and enjoy the woman's company immensely.

The printer sprang to life and started printing out invoices, and Jennie came over so that Rachel could give her a crash course in computer operation.

"That doesn't seem too bad," Jennie admitted, after Rachel had made her open and close the program a few times. "Thanks, Rachel."

"No problem." And Rachel meant it. Jennie was so sweet, how could she not want to help her?

"I'm sorry you're stuck here so late. I tried to cancel all the afternoon appointments, but it was too late."

Rachel grinned. "That's okay. I'd hate for poor Tootsie to have to come here twice." Poor Tootsie was Mr. Bedford's temperamental prize Persian cat who had made it clear with her howls that she had better things to do than visit the vet.

"I did manage to get hold of Derek. Bless his heart, he let me reschedule a jaunt out to his place that he booked months ago. But it would have kept poor Garrett out for hours."

"Derek? Why doesn't he use a local vet?"

Jennie looked at her like she'd come from Mars. "This is local, hon."

"Doesn't Derek live in Austin?" Rachel asked, already seething because she was sure she knew the answer.

"Goodness, no. He lives on seventy acres about ten minutes away."

"So he commutes to the city?"

Again, Jennie shook her head. "As far as I know, he

only goes to the city to work with those kids." She frowned at Rachel. "Why?"

"Nothing." She bent back over the computer, trying to look busy.

He'd lied. Garrett had flat-out lied to her when he'd said Derek lived and worked in Austin. The realization sat like a stone in her gut. She'd trusted him, and he'd lied so that he could sabotage her plan.

Of course, it had been an idiotic plan, but that really wasn't the point. The point was, he'd intentionally deceived her. She grimaced, knowing she was grasping for an excuse—any excuse—to salvage her heart.

Behind her, Jennie remained silent for so long that Rachel finally twisted in her chair.

"Is something wrong?" Rachel asked, wondering if Jennie had read her mind.

"I just want to apologize."

Wary, Rachel nibbled on her lip. "For what?"

"For Carl," she said, and Rachel suddenly felt cold. "He told me this morning what happened at school."

"Oh." Rachel could only stare, her eyes wide open.

Jennie took her hand. "He wanted to apologize in person, but Garrett suggested he wait." She looked at Rachel over the rim of her glasses. "I understand there was some confusion?"

"A comedy of errors."

One corner of her mouth lifted. "Garrett punched him, you know."

Rachel blinked at the non sequitur, then Jennie's words hit home. "As in *hit?* Why?"

"You, of course."

The pronouncement warmed Rachel right down to her toes, and she didn't give a damn how politically incorrect that might be. Garrett had slugged his brother. For her.

How romantic.

She frowned, trying to reconcile the man who'd lied to her with the man who'd protected her honor even against his own brother. *They're the same. Didn't he make you realize how absurd your plan was? Isn't that chivalrous in a backwards sort of way?*

Maybe. She nibbled on her lip. Okay, *probably.*

No, *definitely.* She did trust him. Implicitly. It was stupid and foolhardy, maybe, but that was how she felt. And, Lord knows, she'd never shied from stupid and foolhardy.

Jennie pulled a stack of patient files from the wire basket. "So tell me about you and Garrett," she said, her voice just a little too casual.

"There's nothing to tell. Garrett's great. I like him a lot." That was the understatement of the year.

"You can do better than that, can't you? After all, he did punch my son for you."

Rachel frowned with the realization that she *could* do better than that. Her feelings for Garrett ran a hell of a lot deeper than a tepid little *like.* Hell, she was in love with the man.

Love?

She took a deep breath, then let it out slowly, testing the emotional waters.

Yes, love. *It was true.* Oh, Lord, it was really true. She'd been dancing around reality, avoiding the truth staring her right in the face.

She loved him, and he didn't even know her, certainly couldn't love her. Not really. Not *her.*

Wasn't that just the pits?

THE FRONT DOOR swung shut behind Ephran Booker and Gigi, his wife's prize pig, as they left. "That's the last of them," Rachel said. "I never realized how busy a vet could get."

"I really appreciate your help," Garrett said, noticing the little lines around her eyes. "You look tired."

"I didn't sleep a lot last night."

Duly noted. But he didn't comment. Not yet.

"Can I buy you dinner?"

"I don't know—"

"I really think we need to talk. You made me a promise, remember? I told you I wanted to see the real Rachel, and you agreed."

She looked up at him, eyes watery. "The deal's off. I told you that last night. It was a stupid plan." She sighed, then tried to smile but did a lousy job of it. "I loved every minute with you, and I really appreciate your help—"

"Rachel—" He tried to interrupt, not liking the direction she was heading.

"No, let me finish. I've sort of rehearsed this."

Rehearsed? That didn't sound good, but Garrett kept silent. If she wanted to make a speech, he'd let her. And when she was done, he'd tell her he loved her.

"If it wasn't for you I probably would have gone through with my ridiculous scheme." She shook her head. "It was a stupid plan—you were right about that. It wasn't Jason or Derek or Carl or even Braemer. It was me." She shrugged. "Forgive and forget, right?"

His heart clenched, but she kept going.

"I'm not going to go to the reunion. There's no point anymore. I'm going to load my car, and then tomorrow I'm heading home."

"You're leaving?" He couldn't have felt worse if he'd been slammed by a two-by-four.

She sighed. "I've got to. No apartment, remember? I have to pack my stuff, find a new place to live."

"Sweetheart, no." He took her hand and looked into her eyes, hoping that if he looked deep enough into those brown pools she'd recognize the truth when he spoke it. "Don't leave. Stay with me. Give us a chance." He took a breath. Now or never. "Rachel, I'm in love with you."

She gasped a little and stepped back, her eyes wide, as if she were seeing something beautiful and amazing—like the Eiffel Tower or the Northern Lights—for the very first time. Then her face clouded, the expression fading, and she dropped her gaze to the floor.

"You don't love me, Garrett." She looked up at him, then. "I really wish you did, but you don't."

"You're wrong."

"You don't even know me." She started pacing the length of the reception hall. "The woman you see isn't me."

He met her on the next pass through the room, taking her hands and pressing them to his chest.

She trembled under his touch, wanting so much to lean against him, to soak up his strength, to stay with him forever and forget all her problems.

"I'm looking right at you," he said. "Tell me what I see."

"The woman who seduced you in the truck and the clinic. But that's not me. I'm not a seductress. It's a mask. I'm good at the act, but that's all it is. A game, a defense mechanism."

"A defense against what?"

"Against the world. Against what the world sees."

She lifted a shoulder, wishing she could make him understand, wishing she were different so this could be easier. Wishing she could believe that he really loved *her*.

He pressed his palm against her face, and she sighed. "I'll tell you what I see," he said, and she held her breath, wondering...*hoping*.

"I see a woman gutsy enough to come all the way back to her hometown to fight her demons." She swallowed, and he went on. "I see a sexy, sensual woman who can turn me on with little more than a look."

Her heart clenched. That wasn't her. "No, that's not—"

"Only me." He kissed her cheek, and she realized he'd kissed away a tear. "You're my seductress, Rach. *Mine*. And you do turn me on more than any other woman—in hospital scrubs as much as in that sexy little black skirt."

The tears came in earnest now, and she wiped them away with the back of her hand.

"I see a shy woman, not really sure she ever left the unattractive little girl behind." He let his eyes graze over her, and her body burned under his steady gaze. "But I assure you she has. She's shy enough to blush when I undress her, and aggressive enough to know exactly what she wants. She's got loads going for her, but she's about a quart low in the self-confidence department. She's witty, and sharp, and she rescues stray dogs, and she's generous enough to give up entire afternoons to organize someone else's filing."

He paused, his forehead creasing as he lifted his brows. "Sound like anyone you know?"

She shook her head, too stunned to speak.

"No? Shall I go on?"

"No." Closing her eyes, she sighed. "Mrs. Kelley was right. You do see a lot."

"Stay with me, Rachel."

"I need—"

The phone rang and she picked it up, the message on the other end giving her chills. She passed him the receiver, wanting to comfort him, wanting to help, but not knowing how. "It's Jennie," she said. "It's about your dad."

When he hung up the phone, his face was grim. "This isn't over, Rachel. Don't leave me without thinking about what I said. And don't you dare leave without saying goodbye."

"I'm coming with you." She needed to be there for him, wanted to offer whatever comfort she could.

"Thank you." He stroked her cheek. "But I think I need to go alone." He flashed a sad smile. "I've got a few demons of my own to confront. Okay?"

She nodded, realizing she was crying again. For a woman who never cried, she'd managed to leak buckets over the past few days.

His finger grazed over her lips. "Let me love you, Rachel. Stay here and let me prove to you that I do. I don't want to star in Garrett Meets the Barbie-Doll-Mata-Hari-Sex-Kitten from Outer Space. I just want you."

"Garrett, I—"

"Shhh," he said, putting a finger on her lips. "Not now. Tomorrow. Meet me at our house tomorrow at noon, okay?"

She nodded.

"Do you promise?"

Their gazes locked, and she knew she couldn't let him down. She wasn't sure what she would say to him, but she'd be there. "I promise."

"WHAT'S WRONG with his heart?" Garrett demanded, the second Jennie opened the door.

"There's not a damn thing wrong with my heart," Carl Sr. said from the living room. Garrett followed the voice, finding his dad in a recliner, a videotape of last year's Super Bowl playing silently on the television.

"He didn't think you'd come unless you thought something was seriously wrong," Jennie explained.

Garrett cast his gaze toward the ceiling. "That's the dumbest thing I ever heard. If you'd just asked me to come, I would have."

"Your mother was unreliable. Took off one day and never came back."

Instead of snapping back that he wasn't his mother and never had been, Garrett held his tongue. No sense giving the old man a heart attack when he didn't already have one. Besides, hadn't he just spent days trying to convince Rachel to forgive and forget? Maybe he'd do well to follow his own advice.

"I hear you've got a damn fine clinic in Los Angeles."

"It's on a ranch in the Malibu Canyon. But thanks."

"Appreciate you showing up here, boy."

Showing up? "No problem."

"Probably was tough leaving a place like that, even for a little while."

Garrett felt his heart quicken, and tried not to guess where the conversation was heading. "Not too tough. The practice is getting a little stale." He took a deep breath, trying to fuel his courage. "I miss working in a small-town clinic. Even on a ranch in Malibu, it's just not the same."

"I hear California's a nice place."

"So's Texas."

His father nodded. "The thing is, I'm getting up in

years. Can't handle the clinic like I once could, and I sure can't handle the calls. Pulled my back out the last time I traipsed through Marjorie Walker's back forty." He turned slightly, shifting his gaze from Garrett to the television, the picture of nonchalance. "I was thinking maybe I could use some help."

"Sounds like you could," Garrett agreed, still holding back, not certain enough where the old man was going.

"Was thinking maybe you'd be interested."

The words were spoken mildly, but the meaning was clear. His dad really did want him there. Wanted Garrett, the vet, anyway. Maybe in time, he'd want Garrett, the son, too.

Garrett nodded, trying to match his father's tone. Better not to rock the boat. They'd reached some sort of uneasy truce, here. Probably best not to yell at the man for being a bastard for almost twenty years. And probably not a good idea to throw his arms around his father, kiss him on the cheek, and tell the old geezer he'd missed him.

Better just to stay cool.

"I'd be interested. Sure."

Only then did his dad turn and smile. "Well, sit down, son. Have a beer and watch some highlights with me."

Later, Garrett stumbled onto the front porch and settled into the swing, shaking his head. He'd just watched two quarters with his father as if they'd been on the best of terms for the past twenty years.

Garrett chuckled as Carl sat next to him.

"The old man apologize?" Carl asked.

"Nope."

"Did he say he wanted your help?"

"Not really."

Carl glared at him. "Come on, man. Jennie told me

he's selling you half the clinic. He must have said something."

"You know, he really didn't say much at all."

"Then why are you in such a good mood?"

Garrett just shrugged and took a long swallow of beer. "I always figured we'd have to start somewhere. And it looks like the old man took the first step."

"Guess my plan worked after all."

Garrett turned, a nagging sense of dread in his stomach. "Plan?" Apparently, everybody in Braemer was working a scheme.

"To get you back home."

"*Your* plan."

Carl shrugged. "It worked."

Slowly, Garrett nodded, the pieces falling together. "Dad never asked for me to come back and help, did he? He just assumed I showed up out of the blue."

"Well, he did say he could use some help around the place. And a couple of times he's mentioned that he's impressed with the reputation you've built." Carl shrugged. "I wanted you home. Jennie wanted you home. And even though he wouldn't admit it, Dad wanted you home. I took a chance."

Garrett almost chuckled. Once again, his baby brother had gotten exactly what he wanted. But he couldn't be angry. Not at all. He was too damn happy to have a reason to stay.

Now if he could just convince Rachel to stay with him, Garrett figured he could mark this down as one of the better months in his life.

HE LOVED HER. She stroked Thumper's coat and let the words flow through her. *He really loved her.*

She'd repeated the mantra all last night, rolling the realization around in her head, letting it melt and sift down to flavor every part of her. Perched on the bottom step in the old farmhouse, she hugged her knees to her chest, imagining Garrett there with her, and wondering what she was going to say when he got there.

The sun streamed through the windows, dust dancing in the beams of light. Rachel watched the show, letting her mind drift. Part of her—no, almost all of her—wanted to stay with him, believed he loved her, and loved him right back. A tiny, obstinate part refused to believe. She kept trying to beat that part into submission, but, like something out of a *Friday the Thirteenth* movie, it kept popping back to life.

Footsteps on the front porch rang out like shots. Thumper stumbled to his feet and barked once as she stood up. *Garrett*. The door pushed open and she took a step forward, craving his touch, desperate for him to convince her to stay.

Then he stepped into the hall. Not Garrett.

Carl.

Thumper growled, and Rachel put a calming hand on his head. The growl turned to a low whine.

"Hi, Rachel," he smiled, weak and unsure. "You must be Thumper," he said to the dog.

"Where's Garrett?"

Carl glanced at his watch. "He's coming. It's only eleven-thirty." Carl shoved his hands into his pockets and shifted his weight from one foot to the other, so he ended up swaying in front of her like a little boy. "I...uh...wanted to talk to you."

She waited for the anger and hurt to fill her, but nothing came. Somehow, when she wasn't looking, she'd forgiven Carl and released the hurt. "It's okay," she said, knowing the words were true. Now she just wanted to move on.

"No, it's not. I was an ass. You were my friend and I should have stood up to Jason. I should never have let him bully me into abandoning you at the prom. I should have beat the hell out of him for even thinking about giving you grief. I was a total and complete jerk, and I've owed you an apology for ten years."

He looked so intense, so sincere, that she couldn't help the smile that tugged at her mouth. "Yes, you were. Apology accepted."

"If it's any consolation, I'm not a jerk now. Ask anyone." He grinned. "Well, almost anyone."

"You *were* a jerk. But a lot of it was me, too. I saw the town and everyone in it as enemies." She shrugged, remembering all the people who'd welcomed her during the past few days. "It turns out I was wrong."

He nodded. "Are you going to the reunion tonight? I'd really appreciate it if you'd agree to dance with me."

"No. Thanks, but I'm not going." She bit her lower lip.

Moving past her, he headed for the steps, keeping a watchful eye on Thumper, then sat down. Thumper settled between them, and Carl tentatively patted the dog's rump.

"He loves you," Carl said.

She traced a pattern on the dusty handrail, her other hand lost in the comfort of Thumper's fur. "So he says."

"You sound unconvinced."

"I just wonder if he sees the real me." She turned to face him, wanting to explain what was bugging her, but not sure how to put it into words. "I'm not the together woman I show to the world. I've got tons of insecurities, and every single one of them has kept popping back on this trip. I keep slipping back into Belinda Rachel, and I don't want to be that girl again." She sighed. "But I'm terrified she's who I really am."

"Yeah? Well, I knew her in high school and liked her. She was overly shy, but a real sweet girl."

She snorted.

"Did it ever occur to you that you've changed, too?"

She frowned. Obviously he wasn't listening. "I've just told you I don't think I have. It's Belinda all over again."

"So? Maybe Belinda's grown up. I've changed, Derek's changed—why can't you believe you've changed, too? Maybe the person Garrett fell in love with is the real you. A few pieces of Rachel, a few pieces of Belinda—"

"Stir and make a real woman?" she said, joking, but considering what he was suggesting.

"Sure. Why not?"

"Jason hasn't changed," she said, not ready to believe.

"If you're going to use Jason as a mile-marker, we're never going to get there. He was a jerk then, he's a jerk now. And trust me, he *has* changed. He's an even bigger jerk now."

"You really think Garrett's in love with me? The real me?"

"I'm sure of it. But if you're not, there's only one way to find out."

She lifted a brow.

"Stay in Braemer a few more days. Figure it out yourself."

Could it really be true? She thought back over all the times she'd been with Garrett, all the times she hadn't worried about whether or not she was playing the role to the hilt. She'd started out in the role of seductress, true, but it never completely stuck. Somehow, with Garrett, the hard edges of her persona kept getting worn down. He'd said he wanted the real Rachel, and she hadn't believed him.

But maybe it really was true. Everything he did, everything he said, suggested Carl was right. And she wanted so much to believe.

She nibbled on her lip. "I'll stay," she finally said. No matter what, she loved Garrett. And Garrett said he loved her, too. The thought warmed and filled her. She'd stay and figure it out. Garrett was worth putting her heart on the line.

She met Carl's eyes and smiled, two friends sharing a moment. Then the moment was shattered by a *thunk* near the kitchen. Thumper barked, the sound echoing through the empty hall. Rachel shushed him, then turned to Carl.

Frowning, he stood up. "Stay here."

She nodded, telling herself not to be nervous. Probably just an animal. Standing, she watched Carl disappear. Then Thumper growled, and a chill ran down her spine when she realized she wasn't alone.

"Hello, Belinda."

Spinning around, she faced Jason, his pretty-boy face distorted with malice. She held her hand down, silently willing Thumper to stay calm.

"What are you doing here?"

"I finally remembered where I'd seen you," he said, calmly taking a step toward her. "And hasn't little Belinda grown up in all the right places?"

Terror swept over her and she backed away, Jason matching her every step until the decorative end of the banister pressed painfully between her shoulder blades.

"If you're going to flirt like that, little lady, you need to be prepared to follow through." He smiled and reached out a hand to trace her cheek, and she shivered with revulsion. "Just in case someone else hasn't already, I'm gonna make sure the prediction doesn't come true." He leaned forward, his breath hot and threatening against her. "I'm going to make sure you don't die a virgin."

Anger whipped through her. She was through taking any crap from this creep. Drawing on all her strength, she slammed her palms against him, catching him off guard and making him stumble back. "Get away from me."

"Little bitch." Rage burned in his eyes, and he took another step toward her.

Run. She twisted, heading toward the kitchen, but he caught the back of her shirt and pulled her back. She screamed, and then suddenly she broke free and Jason was howling. She whipped around to see him kick Thumper, his boot toe catching the dog squarely in his bandaged hindquarter.

"No!" she yelled as Thumper went sliding across the floor. She leapt on him, prepared to pummel him, but he caught her arms, twisting them painfully behind her back.

"Get off her." Carl's voice was even, determined, but Jason just sneered.

"Stay out of this, MacLean. This is between me and the lady."

"The hell it is."

Then Carl rushed him, landing a punch in his upper arm. Rachel twisted free, rubbing her arm, and kicking uselessly at Jason. Carl may have been a hell of a football player ten years ago, but now he was a lawyer, and no match for a man who looked like he bench-pressed buses.

"Look out!" she yelled, but Jason caught Carl against the jaw and he went down.

Hell.

"Hold it right there, Jason," Garrett said.

She spun around, then ran behind Garrett, who stood stock still, a shotgun aimed at Jason.

"You okay?" Garrett asked.

She nodded, burying her face against the back of his shoulder.

"Never better," she mumbled.

BY THE TIME the police had left with Jason in cuffs, Rachel felt a little calmer, and she settled back in the library window seat to watch the black-and-white pull away. Thumper, no worse for wear, rested just below her, a diligent guard, his eyes never leaving her.

Garrett came up and settled in behind her on the window seat, pulling her against his chest. "Feeling better?"

"I'm fine. He scared me, but he didn't hurt me."

He hugged her close and kissed the top of her head as Carl stepped in from the parlor, absently rubbing his jaw. "We should get out of here," Carl said. He looked pointedly at Rachel. "If we're going to the reunion, we need to get cleaned up."

"So, what do you say?" Garrett asked, pulling them both to their feet. "Do you want to go to the dance tonight?"

She looped her arm around Garrett's waist and leaned into him. She drew strength from being beside him, only this time, she didn't need the strength. This time, she'd be fine on her own. "Why not?" she finally said, looking up at the man she loved. She smiled, happier than she could ever remember being. "But your brother owes me the first dance."

"I think I can rein in my jealousy."

They followed Carl out onto the porch, the deep blue of the Texas sky surrounding them, a silent promise for the future.

"There's something I need to tell you," Rachel said, holding Garrett back as Carl walked on to his car.

She took a deep breath and looked him in the eyes. "I love you."

It felt right saying it. *Rachel loves Garrett.* Not Seductress Rachel, not Belinda Rachel. Just Rachel. "I love you," she repeated, then laughed because saying it sounded so nice.

His smile was so smug, she laughed even harder.

"I know you do," he said pulling her against him and kissing her hard. Then he tilted up her chin and looked deep in her eyes. "I love you, too. *You,*" he added, and her heart swelled.

"Come here," he said, then led her down the steps and held her close.

"I really love this place," she said, leaning her head on his chest. Before it had been hers, now it almost felt like *theirs.*

"Me, too." He squeezed her shoulder and kissed the top of her head. "It's been sold, you know," he said blandly. "Someone put a contract on it just this morning."

"Our house?" No way. Unacceptable. She leaned back so she could get a look at him, trying to remember enough real property law to convince him that they could somehow break the contract.

Then she saw his mouth twitch.

"What?" she said, her heart picking up its tempo. *Don't jump to conclusions. You'll only be disappointed.* "Why are you smiling?"

"You didn't ask *who* bought the house."

She nibbled on her lower lip. "I'm afraid to guess wrong."

The smug grin returned. "Then I'll just tell you. I'm buying it." He kissed the tip of her nose. "For us."

Us? Her heart beat faster and her skin tingled. "Is that a proposal, Dr. MacLean? Because I don't see you down on one knee."

He stroked her cheek. "Not a proposal, per se, sweetheart. More like an open offer. I don't want to pressure you. If you want me, let me know. I'll end up on one knee so fast it'll make your head swim." He winked. "The ball's in your court, Rach."

"The last time I heard that, I lasted about fifteen minutes before I started throwing things at the ceiling." She wrapped her arms around his neck, bringing her mouth close to his ear. "This time, I'm shooting for at least twenty."

_____Epilogue_____

RACHEL WIPED HER HANDS on her jeans, leaving a trail of peach paint down her thighs. "We're never going to be finished in time."

"Nonsense," said Paris, "we've still got six days until the wedding."

All around her, the entrance hall of the old Duncan farmhouse—soon to be the MacLean house—stood proud but half-painted. The only decoration was the giant Christmas tree, cans of paint, rollers and brushes spread out below it like presents. Martha Stewart would not approve.

"This is all Garrett's fault," she said, and it was true. "This is all your fault," she hollered out the front door, just for good measure. Not that she really cared. They could get married in the dusty cellar and she'd be happy.

Garrett rushed through the doorway with a hammer. Carl and Devin followed at his heels, each with a tool belt jangling.

"Are you okay?" Garrett asked, concern shining in his eyes.

"We're fine," she said, immediately feeling guilty for having worried him. "Promise."

As soon as the anxiety drained from his face, she rolled her eyes and grinned at Paris, who just shrugged.

"Men," Paris said, as Devin swung an arm around her waist.

"I was just saying that this is all your fault," Rachel explained

"Oh." Garrett looked toward Devin and Carl, who both looked befuddled. "What is?"

"Well, I was talking specifically about the fact that we don't have time to finish the house before the wedding—"

"We'll get it done," said Paris.

"—but the statement applies pretty much across the board." She rubbed a hand over her stomach, grinning, still not quite able to believe it was true. "This little scrapper's your fault, too, and I swear he keeps kicking."

"It's only been three months," said Carl. "Do they kick that soon?"

"Either that or the enchiladas didn't sit well. The point is, the house isn't ready for a wedding. But your brother insisted on getting married before Christmas."

"I insisted?" He sauntered over and pulled her into his arms. "I seem to remember a bride-to-be who wanted to fit into her dress."

"Well, that's true." She looked at Paris. "It's a Nina Ferelli original. The dress alone's worth getting married for." She leaned against Garrett who wrapped his arms around her. "Of course, he's worth at least two of the dresses."

"Only two?" Garrett asked.

"Maybe more," Rachel admitted. "Ask me later tonight."

Paris looked at Devin. "See? I told you marriage wouldn't change her."

No, Rachel thought. It wouldn't change her at all.

Somehow in the past ten years she'd become the woman she wanted to be, and then she'd been lucky enough to find a man willing to peel through all her layers until he found that woman buried underneath. The woman who'd finally learned to just be herself. Especially with the man she loved.

She glanced at the mantle and the polished trophy sitting proud above the fireplace. She grinned, remembering how Carl and the reunion's award committee had presented Derek with his trophy. Then Carl had presented her with the matching award, and her breath had caught as she read the inscription—*The Girl Most Changed Since High School.*

"I love you, Rachel Dean." Garrett pulled her close, her back against his chest, his chin resting on her head, and she knew with absolute certainty that he always would.

"That's Rachel Dean MacLean to you, thank you very much," she said, then looked at her watch. "At least it will be in six days, seven hours and fifteen minutes."

He kissed her hair. "But who's counting?"